The Zyratron Affair

The Zyratron Affair

Joe Nowlan

[signature]

Oak Tree Press Hanford, CA

Oak Tree Press
Publishers Since 1998

THE ZYRATRON AFFAIR, Copyright 2013, by Joe Nowlan, All rights reserved. Printed in the United States of America. No part of this book may be used or reproduced in any manner whatsoever without written permission except in the case of brief quotations used in critical articles and reviews. For information, address Oak Tree Press, 1820 W. Lacey Boulevard, Suite 220, Hanford, CA 93230.

Oak Tree Press books may be purchased for educational, business or sales promotional purposes. Contact Publisher for quantity discounts

First Edition, October 2013

ISBN 978-1-61009-104-6
LCCN 2012934513

The Zyratron Affair is dedicated to my niece,
Kathryn Grace Nowlan.

Acknowledgements

Thanks and appreciation for the feedback, corrections and critical brickbats to Victoria Fraza Kickham, Joyce McDevitt, Kat McDevitt and Mark Russell.

Author's Note

The irony is not lost on me re: the novella-esque length of *The Zyratron Affair*.

I can watch a three-hour movie and remain engrossed. And I have no complaints when a baseball game takes three-and-a-half or four hours to complete.

Nonetheless, I admit that *The Zyratron Affair* is not *Atlas Shrugged*-like in its page count.

Why? Because that's how long this story is.

I refer you to man for whom the overused cliché is nonetheless apt: the late, great Elmore Leonard, who was often quoted as saying, "When you write, try to leave out all the parts readers skip."

Now my quoting Elmore Leonard may be a bit like Miley Cyrus singing "Like a Rolling Stone."

But I looked to his comments as a prototype re: *The Zyratron Affair*.

CHAPTER 1

Wednesday, April 11

When you think about it, life can often be seen as a series of what ifs.

What if Michael Jordan had stopped growing at 5'6"? What if Thomas Edison had said, "This light bulb thing's a loser. I'm going fishing." What if Noah had said, "Just a passing shower. It'll be over soon."

And while perhaps not as historically significant ... What if Linda Hamilton wasn't having a birthday, and what if she wasn't a big fan of tongue-in-cheek, kitschy gifts, then I wouldn't have been in the Yesterday & Forever store staring at a dead body whose distinguishing characteristic was a caved in skull over the left ear.

The body—male, maybe 60 years of age or so—was lying face up, next to a four foot high table on which was a notebook, a calculator and a telephone. The store specialized in collectible toys from the '50s, '60s and '70s. Looking around the seemingly empty store, I damn near tripped over the body. My foot kicked his as I was calling out "Anyone here?" My first reaction was to think, "Here's some poor guy with a hole in his head and I'm asking him for help. I'm real good today."

For what it's worth, he had on a pair of brown corduroy pants, a white shirt now a bit bloody around the collar, and a black vest. I noticed a pair of glasses a few feet away from his head. I had met the guy before.

Behind the counter on the floor was one of those old, tin lunch pails which was now severely dented and quite bloody. I think it was what the boys in homicide would call the murder weapon. One of the lunch pail's sharp, pointed corners was rounded off. It also had a small piece of scalp and dried, caked blood stuck to it. Christ...

A duller mind than mine might have thought to call the consumer protection crowd and report a dangerous toy. Not me.

And a weaker stomach—like I used to have—might have turned queasy. Not anymore.

I took out my cell, hit 911, and asked them to come look at a body at the Yesterday & Forever store on Columbus Avenue, Boston, Massachusetts, USA.

As I hung up the phone, I saw a Man from U.N.C.L.E gun and shoulder holster set hanging on a wall hook about six feet away. I watched the re-runs on cable as a kid and could remember that one agent was named Napoleon Solo. The other was Illya something or other. You remember the damndest things sometimes.

The Zyratron Affair

By the time I could recall what U.N.C.L.E stood for, the wail of a Boston Police Department siren could be heard. Louder and louder, closer and closer.

Maybe one of them could remember Illya's last name.

My name is Ben Hudson, and I'm a photographer for the Boston Banner, a weekly newspaper.

I was off the Wednesday that I went into Yesterday & Forever and found what I found. Now they say that a news photographer is never really "off" and I can see the theoretical point there. But "they" have never tried to find a parking space in Boston's South End. So, ever the street-smart dude, I took the subway and a bus to the store. Camera-less. Hey, I was shopping.

Thus it was that about 20 minutes after the police arrived, I, Ben Hudson, was the only photographer on the scene. Scoop city? Nay, nay. I was there without any equipment, not even a lens cap.

A familiar face, although the name took me a few seconds, came forward. "You again?" said a stern but not too unpleasant man in a suit. Homicide detective Bruce Cowley and I had worked together previously, I guess you could say.

A year or so ago, a very beautiful TV news reporter was the one nailing, sexually as well as murderously, a few Boston media folks. She was nailing (sexually) me, when her unique approach to dating was uncovered. Never did find out whether I was due to enter her second phase of nailing. Just as well. In a number of ways, she qualified as drop dead gorgeous, and let's leave it at that.

"You still taking pictures, Ben?" Cowley asked. I wasn't sure if he was just making small talk or starting to question me. Both, I figured.

"Hell, I come in to buy an overpriced lunch pail and a murder breaks out," I said.

"Whaddya know?" Cowley said. I told him, ending with "and I touched nothing except the doorknob." I hoped that didn't sound too much like "What a good boy am I."

At that point, it was a little after 11 a.m. A medical examiner was now giving the corpse the once over. I heard him tell Cowley something or other, which ended with "hour and a half or so." How long he'd been dead, I guessed.

After I gave the statement and everything, Cowley left it that he'd be in touch with me, if necessary. As I left the store, I saw a small crowd—maybe 10 or 15 people.

I was still ticked I didn't have a camera with me, though. Now, it wasn't as if this meant the Pulitzer. And even if I had my equipment, I just wasn't the type to take a shot of the guy with his skull caved in. I don't have much in the way of professional standards but that would be too much even for me. Not sure who'd print it anyway; some bizarre web site, maybe?

So even if I had my equipment, all I'd be really getting was a standard shot of a body bag being removed from the store. Just the same, I couldn't help feeling like a hockey player who had lost his stick.

But I'm getting ahead of myself. Seeing a dead body

will do that. Actually, this all started to unfold...

...Six Days Earlier, Thursday, April 5

I was photographing a grown man as he held a Herman Munster doll in one hand and a Gunsmoke lunch box in the other. I shot him from two different angles. It was a tossup as to whether he looked as silly as I felt.

He wore a dark suit with purple pin-stripes. Purple. Not violet or lavender or some art school expression. Purple. White shirt with a pink necktie. I couldn't tell if it was a clip on. Somehow he made it work.

His name, I swear, was Giuseppe GePetto, owner and proprietor of Yesterday & Forever, a used toy store—or rather a "collectible toys" shop, as he phrased it.

I was wearing neither purple nor pink. But plenty of black, I admit. You can't get into the photographers union without wearing all black two days a week.

Linda Hamilton, a reporter for the *Banner*, was interviewing GePetto for an article she was doing on old toys and their soaring value among collectors.

"But you can't be too careful sometimes," GePetto was telling her. "Why I had someone in here last week who tried to negotiate with me for this Herman Munster doll. He had the temerity to say to '$125 and that's as high as I go.'" GePetto smirked as if the guy had offered him magic beans. He held Herman in his left hand. "This Munster doll—one of maybe a few dozen known to still exist—commanded $500 at a recent Sotheby's auction."

He paused, looking proudly at Herman. "Sotheby's, if you don't mind."

I took a few more shots of him as well as several of his shop and its various displays of memorabilia. A few customers, three or four, maybe, were scattered about the store.

Those old tin lunch boxes were very big among collectors, he had said earlier. Laid out on a couple of tables was practically an entire day's programming on the re-run channels. Dennis the Menace; Mr. Ed; Patty Duke; F-Troop and, wearing a $650 price tag, Lost in Space—which is both the name of the TV show and, I'd imagine, the intellectual qualification of any would-be buyer.

G.I. Joe and Barbie dolls were on another table. Also, the Lone Ranger and a few superhero types I couldn't identify. Several board games were stacked on a nearby shelf including a Beatles "Flip Your Wig" game. Released pre-Sgt. Pepper, no doubt.

Linda was wearing a T-shirt under her blazer. The T-shirt showed a woman wearing either a wedding dress or a prom dress, excuse my lack of fashion sense. The woman was standing in a fountain in a park and somehow remained dry despite the gushing water. Captivating in a way. GePetto seemed to agree.

"I very much like the image you have on your shirt," he said, and you have to give the guy credit. He somehow could say this, looking at Linda's chest, and make it sound non-suggestive, even downright appropriate. If I tried that, I'd be held for psychiatric observation.

"Oh, thanks," Linda said. "It's a beautiful painting, and I still miss being able to see the original."

"Yes, the Windsor Museum has left blank the space where it used to hang," GePetto said. "Hopefully there's a place in one of the rings of hell for the thieves."

While listening to them, I recalled how the image on Linda's T-shirt was of a painting stolen from the Windsor in suburban Boston a few years back, I believe it was. The thieves stole a few paintings, but this was the big one. It was major news here and virtually worldwide, especially in the art world.

I took the press tour of the museum after the robbery, photographing the space where the painting once hung. The space remains blank to this day. The museum's way of leaving a light on for it. I'd really impress myself if I could remember the name of the painting.

"Girl in a Fountain. One of Renaldo Claravecchio's masterpieces," GePetto said, shaking his head a little.

Girl in a Fountain. Got it.

At this point, I was sort of browsing and half listening to GePetto answer Linda's questions. Normally I won't accompany the reporter on a story. I like to simply go in, get the picture, especially if it's just a head and shoulders shot of someone, and be gone. However my car was "in the shop," as they say in the motor industry. Lately, it had been going through brake fluid like a college kid goes through a first credit card. I finally gave in and dropped it off at a mechanic in Dorchester since, on the previous night at about 3 a.m., I applied the brakes at Stuart and Tremont only to have the car keep going, finally coming to a halt about 100 feet past the intersection in front of a pizza joint. Four hookers and a couple of gender-indefinite humans looked up from their food, blinked once, and finished eating.

GePetto and Linda were still talking as I scanned the shop. A McHale's Navy PT boat was priced to move at $75. Elsewhere was an Addams Family glow-in-the-dark ball; a Laurie Partridge doll ($175), a Bewitched magic wand and a Brady Bunch beach towel.

GePetto and Linda shook hands. The interview over, she put back on a beret, black with red polka dots. Standing with the purple and pink GePetto, the two of them looked like figures from the early, blurry days of color television.

"All set, Benjamin?" Linda asked.

"Now, are you going to be at the trade show and auction this weekend?" GePetto asked us. It was the first I'd heard of any auction.

"Yes. I will be swinging by, Mr. GePetto," she said.

"Well, the knockoffs, the imitations are also going to be available from what I understand," GePetto replied. "The way you can tell is to look on the bottom of the left foot. With an original, you'll find a 'Z' engraved on the sole along with three numerals. Not everyone knows this. The counterfeiters never do."

"You will have a booth there?" Linda asked.

"Right next to the Batman exhibit, or so I'm told," he said.

"What time is the auction set for?" Linda asked, as we headed to the door.

"Saturday at five," he replied, adding with what I think was a twinkle in his eye. "Don't forget your checkbook."

"Oh, I'll bring it but at a starting bid of $12,500 you'll need to wait about five years for it to clear," she laughed.

"Wasn't he adorable?" Linda enthused as we walked towards her car. She pointed to a yellow car, a Volkswagen or Fiat or something pretty small, and added, "There's his car. He mentioned it to me. Isn't it cute?"

We walked on to the next block and as we neared her car, I turned to Linda. "I'm afraid to ask but what is it that is starting at $12,500?"

"The Zyratron doll, three of which he purchased in Japan. GePetto estimates there are maybe ten that are known to exist in the whole world, if that many. He's keeping one for himself and auctioning the other two this Saturday. You free to get a picture?"

"Sure," I said. "Man! $12,500 to start! Can you imagine what he'd get if anyone knew what the hell Zyratron was."

"Oh, say it ain't so," she said, visibly and mockingly disappointed. "You don't know Zyratron? I should make you walk home." She opened her car door, got in and leaned over to let me in the passenger side.

"Zyratron," she continued, "was the run amok robot who starred in The Attack of Zyratron, The Return of Zyratron and The Legend of Zyratron. They represented a trilogy of monster flicks made in Japan in the early '60s. Didn't you ever watch bad horror movies as a kid?"

"We were only allowed TV reruns in my house, I

think," I said.

"Those films were absolutely marvelous in their awfulness," she enthused. "The closest thing to a special effect was when they had Zyratron growl, a godawful sound. We'd play drinking games in college and have to down a shot whenever that growl came out. And they had the actors' voices sloppily dubbed in English, the sound poorly synched so their lips would stop moving but words still came out. Hilariously bad. Terrible editing and all."

"Well, yeah I know the type," I said. "But a little of that goes a long way; watching bad movies, I mean. I can't keep my tongue in cheek that long. My mouth gets sore."

"Hmmph. I got Francois Truffaut in my car," she said, stopping for a red light. "I guess they marketed, or tried to market, a line of Zyratron dolls at one time. They never sold but a few have turned up. While in Japan for a recent toy collectors' convention, GePetto managed to purchase three. He won't say what he paid but they'll start the bidding at $12,500, so...."

"But where the bidding ends is what he has to worry about, right?" I said. "He can start the bidding at $12,500 but if the final bid is about 20 bucks, he's not looking too good."

"My birthday is coming up, you know," she said. "A Zyratron doll could make a girl very happy."

"Now I find out," I said. "What is it that women want? Intimacy? Diamonds? Shoes? Nope. Zyratron memorabilia."

CHAPTER 2

Same Day, Six Days Earlier, Thursday, April 5

Later that same day, Linda dropped me off and I returned to the offices of the Boston Banner.

Things were pretty quiet at the offices, as Thursdays often were. The place was less than half occupied. Al Huber's desk was bare, save for an almost empty coffee cup. As the paper's editor, he tended to come in late, if at all, the day after an issue got finished.

Sam O'Neil, managing editor, wasn't at his desk either but I could hear his voice. This wasn't a tribute to his vivid persona so much as the fact that he was emerging from the men's room down the hall. He and Lou Hinton, one of the art directors, then entered the main newsroom continuing a loud but friendly discussion as to who really won the Hagler-Leonard fight.

"Look, I loved Marvin. Tough. Hungry. Never got his due," Lou was saying now as he and Sam came into view. "But the guy got out pointed. Leonard won."

"You don't out point a great champion," Sam came back. "Leonard didn't beat Marvin. He out People-magazined him. He out celebrity-cultured him. He out popularized him. Like Ben Stiller is a more popular actor then DeNiro is how Leonard beat Hagler."

That was an analogy I hadn't heard before. Pretty good one, though. Hinton threw up his hands in mock anger.

"Aarrgh! For this I left The Economist," he grunted.

"The Economist. Yeah," Sam smiled. "And before that, the Kenyon Review." He was back at his desk, waving to me as his phone rang and he picked up to answer.

I headed for what used to be the darkroom I share with Marcus Golden, our other full-time photographer. Now it's a combination man cave and storage closet. Our usual thing is to leave notes for each other—our schedules rarely find us in the offices together—should supplies be running low or what not.

On the counter was a yellow post-it, which stated succinctly: "Rondo!" Our mutually favorite basketball player had a big night against somebody or other. Marcus was a big Rondo fan. Can't blame him, can you?

As I say, it used to be a darkroom. And I still find myself saying "develop" film. Even though you actually upload or download photos now. "Develop" still sounds better to me. Like my grandmother would always called the refrigerator the "icebox."

I stood there for a moment toying with whether or not to download the shots of GePetto. "Toying." Geez, I was getting fed up with this stuff already. With that, the intercom buzzed.

"I'm going to hold a staff meeting in about 15 minutes at Muldoon's," Sam was telling me. "I'd like you to be there to deliver the sermon, Reverend Heineken."

"Yes, rabbi," I said. "Will there be one collection or two?"

"Oh, I would expect at least that many. Maybe three or four collections at this service."

Muldoon's is roughly equidistant, as they say in geometry class, from the offices of the Banner and Fenway Park. When the Red Sox are home, the joint is jammed by, say, five o'clock or so. When they are away on a road trip, you get a few nurses from the hospitals in the area. And then there are the students from Simmons College up the avenue. Ditto from Emmanuel College down the street. Location. Location. Location.

Linda couldn't make it. Hinton had something or other to do, and nobody else was around. So it was Sam and me and the nurses. To the good life.

We sat at the bar. The place had about a dozen or so round tables; half dozen booths, up against the walls, which featured various photos of sports figures and movie stars. There was a fairly good juke box, or whatever they're called now, with a small paneled dance floor in front of it. I ordered a couple of drafts, while Sam went to punch in the two songs he always punches in: Van Morrison doing "Jackie Wilson Said" followed by Jackie Wilson doing "Lonely Teardrops." Symmetry of a sort.

"We should hear them any hour now," Sam said as he sat back down. He was referring to how he usually couldn't stay long enough to get to hear those songs, given the backlog of songs ahead of them.

The song being played at that moment was "The Girl from Ipanema." Two young women were vamping the song—one slinking while she mouthed the lyrics and the other mimed the Stan Getz saxophone part.

"What the hell? Did exam week just get over?" I asked Sam. He shrugged, eyeing the pretend singer.

"Nice voice, though," he commented.

The next song came on: the Supremes doing "Stop in the Name of Love." This resulted in what looked like half the nursing staffs of Boston standing and putting up their hands in a stop sign as they mimicked the Supremes' old stage show.

"Stop signals. God, how original. It's the damnedest thing how this culture of ours forces you to make an effort not to get sick and tired of something great," Sam said, as we turned our chairs towards the TV over the bar. They had some suit coat gesturing in front of a map, giving the weather.

"Oh, they are just blowing off steam at the end of a day of bed pans and life-saving," I said. "Not every patient they get to see undressed is as hunk-like as we are."

"Well, we got bad dancing on one side and TV weather on the other," Sam proclaimed. "It is an absurd metaphor at work, but I'm not sure for what."

"Speaking of absurd," I said, "an original Laurie Partridge doll now goes for $175. For the record."

"For that much, I hope it comes fully inflated," Sam said. He was eyeing another TV, which had been switched over to ESPN showing highlights of some football game from last season.

"And your old Lost in Space lunch box goes for more than I make in a month," I told him. "Try that for an absurd metaphor."

"You win," he said, signaling to the bartender for two more. "That whole collectible thing—if you can keep the bizarro factor at arms length—can be kind of fun in a harmless way. Did Linda say whether she got anything out of the guy there?"

I nodded. "GePetto. Yeah, he seemed pretty talkative and enthusiastic. She's going to check him out at some auction he's holding this Saturday, at that collectors convention."

"Laurie Partridge going to be there?" Sam winked.

"For all I know," I shrugged. "Jesus, he was all hot to trot over these dolls he is going to sell off. He's hoping to get $12,500 or so for something called Zyratron."

"Oh, man. I remember him," Sam laughed. "Or it. Or them. Whichever. Uproariously awful stuff. Zyratron."

I finished my second beer. "Well, evidently there are enough people out there—"

"Hold it," he jumped in. "He's getting twelve-five for one of these, you said? Twelve-five-fucking-thou for a Zyratron doll?"

"I guess they tried to market them years ago when the

Zyratron movies were popular, such as they were ever popular," I said, recalling what Linda had told me. "And they evidently sold in the low dozens. Now there are about a handful left, I guess, and GePetto's got three of them. I think he said he's going to keep one for himself and get all he can for the other two."

We both meditated on all that for a bit. The jukebox was now playing "Strangers in the Night."

"There is a certain consistency there, when you think about it," Sam eventually said. "In a country where a pitcher with a bad arm can earn $10 million and you have to wait an hour for your selection to come out of the jukebox, I suppose a Zyratron's worth about $12,500."

He sipped his beer. "Zyratron." Sip. "Twelve-thousand-five." Sip. "Capitalism can be a strange beast sometimes."

A Door's song came over the juke. Sam grunted. "Wrong Morrison, kids."

CHAPTER 3

***Present day, Saturday, April 14,
three days after GePetto's murder***

While it had been only a couple of days since GePetto was killed, life went on, as it usually does.

So they were holding the seventh annual Toy Collectors and Appreciators Guild Show & Auction at the Park Plaza Hotel in Boston. It's a pretty nice hotel, about a block from the Public Garden, which is very nice, especially in the spring. It's also about a block or so from the Four Seasons Hotel, which is very, very nice. It gets a "two very" rating because everyone from Axl Rose to Hillary Clinton stays there. A "pretty nice" represents a more moderate price level. More to the point, the Park Plaza's main ballroom is big enough to hold anything this side of Alpine skiing.

On this day the place resembled a semi-ornate flea market. It looked like hundreds of tables and booths were set up under the ballroom's crystal chandeliers. I wouldn't say entering the room was like crossing to the other side of the looking glass; more like getting stuck in the middle.

Had it been laid out chronologically, the whole room could have represented a child's cultural upbringing, circa 1960s through the mid-'70s or so. You had a Partridge Family look-alike group scheduled to perform on the main stage. Among the various animated figures represented were three or four guys dressed up as Popeye. Along with an uncharacteristically well-endowed Olive Oyl.

A guy who was supposed to resemble Mr. Magoo was stumbling around as a near blind man would—actually getting laughs and giggles as in his stumbling about, he would "accidentally" grab some woman by the rear. Magoo does that and he gets giggles. It would be Miranda Rights time for me, if I ever tried it. Celebrities get all the breaks.

Various blasts from the past such as F Troop and the Lone Ranger were floating around. A large sign at one table read "Due to scheduling and licensing conflicts, Bugs Bunny, Daffy Duck and Tweety Bird are not represented at this show. Management regrets the inconvenience."

If you remember the original Play-Doh or Lincoln Logs, you'd have found some here. In addition, there were enough Star Trek-related booths and figures for the next several Trekkie generations. As for Ken and Barbie—well, I guess it's all in the casting. One of the "Kens" looked more like Elvis from the later years, and a

"Barbie" try-to-look-alike had orthopedic shoes and the beginnings of a mustache.

I was just sort of floating around, taking a few pictures here and there. To my left, I saw two Batman figures (Batmen?). One was dressed like the TV Batman, the other as the movie version. Each was viewing the other with a look-down-your-mask expression. Behind me a voice said, "This could bring back LSD, couldn't it?"

I turned to see a man with a droopy, almost walrus-like mustache, shaggy black hair, blue jeans and a black, long-sleeved T-shirt that had "Down Highway 61" on the front. I caught a quick glimpse of a tattoo on his left forearm, but couldn't be sure what it was. Compared to the overall surroundings, he almost looked like something out of a Brooks Brothers catalog.

He giggled a little. "I keep wanting to reach for the clicker." He was stocky, just short of pudgy, not so much like an ex-athlete than an ex-bouncer, perhaps.

"Couldn't they have arranged to bring in a Wonder Woman look-alike for middle aged perverts like me?" he asked me, eyes twinkling and arms outstretched in an exaggerated shrug.

"Or at least, Ginger and Mary Ann," I came back with. This guy had a point. An absurdist sense of humor was essential to get through this scene. He gestured to a table, just to his left.

"Well, I've got a few I Dream of Jeannie magic bottles here. Or perhaps a Morticia Addams doll. Maybe a Love Boat carry-on luggage piece?"

He spoke in a somewhat refined British accent. I

don't know, to me all British accents are pretty refined. And hearing him talk about these old toys and TV items gave the whole subject a bit of an educated, polished intellectual veneer. Like a lot of Americans, that accent immediately makes me want to add 30-to-50 points to the person's IQ. A British accent could say, "Kitchy-kitchy-koo," and I'd immediately think, "Uh, that's Twelfth Night, act three, scene two, isn't it?"

I introduced myself to this guy who, in turn, said his name was Isaac Lynch. He explained to me that he had rented the table at a cost of $100 per day, and figured he stood a pretty good chance of clearing $750-$1,000 for the weekend.

"Okay, surely the whole affair gets more than a little absurd," he said. "Or as I used to say in my hazier days, far out!" He gestured to an item on his table. "This Green Hornet mask went for something like $8.95 back when the show aired, I don't know, in the mid-60s or thereabouts? Because of the movies, today there's this mystique around that show for some people. Also, Bruce Lee played the TV Hornet's sidekick, Kato. This was long before the name Bruce Lee earned international recognition." He took a long pull from a bottle of water. "Some years later, come to think of it, one could say the same about the name Kato."

"So if someone offered you $20, what would it get them?" I asked.

"Two tens," he immediately answered, then laughed. "I fully expect to get maybe $200 for these masks. Honest. I've already had a guy offer $150; says he'll come back later today to see if I'll take it." He just shrugged, adding, "But these knockoff Zyratrons are priced to move, if that helps any."

"I hear they're asking more than $12,000 or so for a real Zyratron at that auction later on," I said, getting my first look ever at one.

"Hey, but these? Twelve bucks a piece," he said, gesturing to his fake Zyratrons. "Such a deal, eh?"

I made a mental note to tell Linda Hamilton about this Isaac Lynch fellow. Not that she ever needed much help from me with her articles, but he seemed like he might make a good interview. Then something on his table caught my eye. Another doll. Or figurine. Whatever they're supposed to be called.

"Is this the Addams Family woman?" I asked, my lack of in-depth familiarity once again revealing itself. I have to watch the re-run channels more often, I guess.

"Morticia. Lovely Morticia," he replied. "Yeah, boy, that was something. Even on black & white telly. She would slink around in that long, clinging black gown of hers." He shook his head in admiration.

Linda once dressed as this Morticia Addams for a Halloween party and looked so sensational that I still keep a photo of her from that night.

"So will $20 give me two tens for Morticia?" I asked, ever the hardball bargainer. "And I'll take a phony Zyratron, too."

He pondered the proposition for a bit. "Sure, let's do it. Always like to stay on the good side of the media. As a wise man once said, 'Never anger a man who owns a printing press.' Oh, and here...." He then put a second knockoff Zyratron in the bag. "Have another one of these. I'll throw it in as a two-fer. Make a good desk ornament."

We made the sale. I told him about Linda perhaps talking to him later and he cheerfully agreed.

"I'm glad someone is buying one of these," Lynch said, pointing to the knock-off Zyratrons. "Even with the publicity about the auction of the originals, the knockoffs haven't found much of a market. Hell, even when Zyratron movies would air on TV, it was never hugely popular. Maybe if the BBC were to do a remake. That might be our best hope."

"I'll give Helen Mirren a call," I said. "She's an old flame."

As I turned to leave, I bumped into a real, live Wonder Woman. Big hair, gold lariat, and, er, all that goes with it.

"That fellow has been asking for you," I said, pointing in Lynch's direction.

"Oh, he has, has he?" Wonder Woman replied, in a voice at least an octave lower than mine.

I walked away hurriedly. Time to get out of the looking glass.

I was strolling up and down the various rows of tables and booths. Action heroes gave way to cartoon characters, and vice versa. Incongruously, a woman in a business suit, carrying a notebook, was also part of the floor show. As I got closer, I saw that her left lapel had a press ID that read "Lois Lane, reporter, Daily Planet." She saw the press badge I was wearing and half smiled at me.

"A journalistic rival, eh?" she said to me.

"No comment, Ms. Lane," I replied. Not bad for me. I'm usually not that smooth.

"If you see Clark Kent, you cutie, tell him I am looking for him," she purred.

She sauntered away and, if I wasn't so smooth, I might have drooled on my lens caps.

Among the various tables and exhibits was a sign in front of a booth area, empty but for a table and chair: "Appearing at 5 p.m., Lori Sinclair, star of TVs 'Wicked Wives' and cast member in the original Zyratron movie. Photos only, please."

She was in Boston at that point to film a movie in our fair city. So the toy show people were able to take advantage of that serendipity, I guess. Next to the table was a then-and-now photo of Lori Sinclair. The first having been taken for the Zyratron movie when she was about six or seven years old from the looks of things. The other was taken for "Wicked Wives." Speaking as a professional photographic specialist, I'd say she grew up and aged very effectively.

Standing next to her booth was a human refrigerator. Or close. He was sort of tanned; maybe European or Middle Eastern. Or Turkish, perhaps. Hell, I'm a big help, aren't I?

Black hair and eyes, broad physique, as I said. A

bodyguard or security guy, I figured. Some of those rugby physiques can turn out to be not so tough after all. More muscle than anything else. Of course, in some lines of work, that's often all you need. Clearly a weight lifter, maybe an ex-football player. Hell, maybe a current football player, at least at a glance. Stayed in shape, that was obvious.

On his left forearm was some sort of tattoo. Ever get the feeling there are about six people left in the world who don't have a tattoo? It was hard to tell with his arms folded but it looked like a semi-circle shaped... something-or-other. I didn't really look for long. It had been a strange enough day already.

I skipped that Zyratron auction, now billed as an auction-memorial dedicated to GePetto, which I doubt made him feel better. I didn't need to watch people richer than I'd ever be throw thousands at something like they were buying two honey dips and a large regular. I had plenty of shots of the various pseudo-action heroes.

Also, what had originally been amusing and entertaining had changed to fairly weird, even fatiguing. In large part due to the fact that I was intermittently puzzled and bemused over one thing. How did I retain all this useless information re: TV-movie and comic book figures—many of them before my time?

I mean, I knew who virtually all these people were (People? Whatever.) And this concerned me. How is it that I actually could retain and recall fairly instantly the distinction between the Green Hornet and Green Arrow? Between the Munsters and the Addams Family? Yet had to think for a bit to distinguish between Mao Tse Tung and Ho Chi Minh—each of whom had a far greater impact on the world overall (if not the toy industry). Let's blame the schools of this country and move on then.

As you have figured by now, I am not always the deepest of thinkers. Yet, the fact was that all this essentially useless minutiae still had a connection in my alleged brain. Then again, if I retained so much of this, could it actually be useless, by definition? Or was it, in point of absolute fact, truly useless and, ergo, made me useless?

All this contemplating my ever harder to find navel made me thirsty so I stopped into a nearby Irish place called M.J. O'Connor's to read and reflect. Since I now had the time, I took one of my replica Zyratrons out of the bag to get my first good look at the thing, save for maybe a quick glance when I was at GePetto's or back at the collectors' show.

While the old movies were in black & white, from what Linda told me, these figurines were color. Guess the producers decided to shoot the works on them. Overall, the thing had a stocky build – maybe a little like a refrigerator with legs. Both the legs had no kneecaps to speak of. They were red and I imagined that when Zyratron walked, it was in a kind of stiff legged gait.

The arms were also red. The body part was silver or gray, take your pick. On the front he wore a rather strange couple of monitors or speedometers; something like that. The needles were painted on and did not move but I suppose were a way for Zyratron to, I don't know, check his own oil, perhaps.

He had yellow eyes centered in round sockets, the size of cocktail coasters. Where ears would be were…hell, I don't know what you'd call them. Antennae-looking contraptions of some sort; like the handles on a slot machine.

It also had a red light on the top of its head, like the light on an older model police car. Well, it's a look, I guess. Most 50 year old fashions either become trendy again or look hilariously outdated. Methinks Brother Zyratron fell into the latter category but didn't seem too fazed by it.

I used to build model cars and airplanes when I was a kid. This Zyratron figurine might have been fun to assemble like that. Any excuse to sniff some glue in those days.

I didn't think I'd attract any attention to speak of but while staring at the Zyratron, the bartender came over and asked, "Is your date there drinking or is she all set for now?"

Kind of summed up my day.

CHAPTER 4

A week later, it was time for Linda's birthday celebration. After a while a few of us in the party couldn't pronounce "celebration" without slurring a consonant or two, if you know what I mean.

For the event, Linda was wearing a candy apple red skirt, matching high heels and purse. She wore a jet black sweater and matching earrings, very large, like poker chips or small hockey pucks. Her '70s phase. Or Mod phase. I never ask anymore.

The name Linda, let alone Hamilton, is common enough. But as luck and our culture's celebrity obsession would have it, she shared the same name with the actress who was in one of Schwarzenegger's Terminator movies. It was a coincidence that had long ago lost its amusement for her, she'd occasionally bemoan.

"'Ah'll be baahhck.' If one more guy says this to me—and does so as if it's the cutting edge of cleverness—I'll perform a surgical procedure on him."

I'm pleased to report my presents went over very well, especially the faux Zyratron on the heels of the Morticia Addams doll. Other birthday goodies from the Banner group included a gift certificate for the tattoo of her choice with both the image and body location left up to Linda. The location became the topic of much dinner conversation—the more liquor that was drank, the more intimate the suggestions became.

Soon the group moved to yet another watering hole for yet another nightcap. In the spirit of knee-jerk Bostonian snobbery, Linda announced. "I wouldn't be seen at Quincy Market on a bet." So we ended up at Los Altos on nearby Broad Street, about a block away. "Okay, but no closher," she slurred eloquently.

The place was packed, leaving only one open seat at the bar into which we steered the birthday girl. As Sam took drink orders, I looked around the room and figured it must have been birthday night in Boston. Four different tables had birthday balloons tied to chairs. Many of these tables were all female, a couple with bouquets of flowers in front of their respective honoree. Most were drinking green or red colored drinks. Cosmopolitans, maybe? Are they still hip? Well, everyone seemed pleased and was tastefully soused, whatever they were drinking.

After Sam and I distributed the drinks and we all performed yet another clinking of glasses, I noticed a familiar face down the bar. I didn't place him at first but

I knew it would come to me—literally, as the face in question had seen me and was coming in my direction.

"Hey, how's the photography business?" he asked, shaking hands. His droopy, walrus-like mustache got me thinking. The British accent clinched it. Sure, the guy from the booth at that toy collectors clambake. It was the damnedest thing. As soon as I heard him talk, his name came to me. God Save the Queen.

"Hi, Isaac. How did that show go for you?" I replied.

"Not bad. After you left I sold a few Bat Masterson card sets. Made more than a couple of bucks for the day," he grinned contentedly. "Hey, so how did the dolls you bought go over?"

At this point Sam was returning with his hands full of more drinks. After doling them out, I made introductions to one and all.

"I can report that the doll went over very well," I told him between sips. "That's the birthday girl over there."

I gestured to Linda, who took that as a sign to join us. She left the bar stool and Groucho-walked over to us.

"This is the doll to whom I gave the doll," I said, with the bravado that only a fourth drink can provide. They remembered each other from the toy collectors show and Linda, who at this point was speaking with what I would call a Smirnoff accent, was saying how "cool the doll will look on my toffee cable...coffee table." She giggled a little. "Wherever the fuck...."

"Couldn't argue with that," Sam laughed. "Hey, I never got a good look at that Zyratron. I was sitting at the far end of the table at the restaurant. Where did you put it, Linda?"

"It's in my Toyota," she purred. "Got a space near the Langham Hotel. With time on the meter. My lucky night."

"Before we call it a night, I'll have to get a look at it," Sam said.

We small talked for 10 minutes or so before Lynch had to leave, promising again to get a copy of the Banner and read the article.

"Wuz he cute?" Linda slurred a few minutes later. "I'm not sober enough to tell."

"I think that's the two-minute warning, gang," Sam announced.

We walked in far-from-straight-lines back to Linda's car, not five minutes away. Sam was the sober, voluntary designated driver so Linda could slur from the shotgun seat and the streets of Boston would be safe to drive. Or as safe as the streets of Boston can be to drive.

Her blue Toyota was parked on a stretch of Oliver Street. As we got within 20 feet of it or so, Linda's voice sobered up instantly, as she said, "Shit, is my trunk closed?"

Sure enough, the car's trunk was ajar just enough to notice. You like to think in that split-second of reflection that Linda had simply not shut the trunk firmly enough. At the same time...we all knew better, I'm afraid.

I once saw some Boston cops pop open a trunk and found quite a mess, consisting primarily of a dead body.

On a positive note, there were no dead bodies here. But the trunk was slightly ajar and someone had gone through it. At first glance, there didn't seem to be anything missing. A couple of gifts Linda had received earlier in the evening were still there. And the bouquet of flowers Sam brought her was also still there.

"Shit, the Zyratron's gone," Linda moaned, in the same tone one would use to exclaim, "My life savings is gone."

It seemed that she was right. Someone had evidentially popped the trunk and smashed, then took, the Zyratron. But part of the torso from the doll was there, but that was it. Yet the thief left behind a bouquet of flowers, a box of Godiva chocolates, the tattoo certificate and an envelope containing another gift certificate to Victoria's Secret. Morticia Addams was still there, too.

"Clearly the work of a sci-fi freak that isn't into ladies underwear and doesn't have a sweet tooth," Sam mused.

CHAPTER 5

The Banner had been having financial troubles of late, along with just about any and every other newspaper in the country. In fact, just about anything involving the word "paper" has been experiencing declining revenues, as they say.

Some of our editions were thinner than others; fewer ads equal fewer pages, you know. So a bit of economic graveyard humor had become more common around the office. People joke about saving soda cans to get the nickel deposit, saving their used tea bags or checking up on their 201Ks. Sometimes everyone really is a comedian. Or tries to be.

But the following week brought with it good reasons to elevate the graveyard humor to Code Worry. The Banner's publisher, Mike Hannah, sent out an e-mail, which set some sort of record for use of "regrettably," "unfortunate" and "great reluctance" before getting around to telling us that The Banner was becoming a free publication. That is, instead of readers paying 50 cents a copy, they would now pay nothing. And, oh yes, a reluctantly reluctant decision to implement across-the-board 20 percent pay cuts. Plus, photographers would henceforth be paid on a per-assignment basis.

It created a strange, cautionary feeling. The cliché "can't give it away" became part of the graveyard humor. I mean, if it's free and readership numbers and advertising revenues still decline … gulp.

"To address our fiscal pain points, we will also offer articles and features as on-line exclusives," Hannah's e-mail added. "This is inevitable in newspaper publishing these days. We want people to link to The Banner's site."

"I call it LLB: "Link Like a Bastard," our fearless leader e-urged. "So be thinking web, people. And ways we can LLB our brand."

Actually, the emphasis on the online version of the Banner made sense and was probably overdue, I guess. Hell, even Sam O'Neil got most of his newspaper reading via the Internet, and he was an old-school newsie who still used a typewriter. Now and then.

"LLB=$$$," Sam wrote in an e-mail reply to me and the rest of our staff.

And added as a P.S., "We hope."

As an immediate reaction to our suddenly—sorry, our

reluctant—fiscal crisis, the Banner staff did not go to a bar. We brought the bar to us; that is, Sam went out and bought a 12-pack.

"To fiscal responsibility," Sam toasted. It was me, Sam and a few others, who stayed around for the afterglow. We tried to discuss our plight with a snobbish sense of tongue-in-check.

"I may have to cancel my fittings with my tailor at Brooks Brothers," I said after a slight belch.

"The Vineyard or Nantucket?" Sam mused. "Certainly can't hit them both this summer, now can we."

Eventually this all deteriorated into longer and longer periods of collective silence. The Banner was founded in the '60s, a time when it was categorized as an "underground newspaper." We now had to worry if that categorization might describe where we end up.

As the semi-wake wound down, Sam and I walked to the subway or the "T" as we locals call it.

"You know it's funny that this all hits the fan now," Sam said as we stood near the subway station entrance. He was heading outbound and I headed for the inbound platforms. "The other day some guy sent me a link to a site looking for freelancers. I looked at the site out of curiosity. After I get home and take an eight hour nap, I'll send it to you. Site claims to be in desperate need of photographers."

"Well, if they're desperate and in need, I guess I'm their boy," I replied.

CHAPTER 6

The e-mail Sam forwarded the next day read: "Photographers needed for two-to-four hour jobs. Must have car and flexible schedule. Note: these jobs are not weddings."

Well, that was good to read. Look, everyone loves weddings except for photographers like me. Some love the challenge, the pressure of getting those vital (for the bride and groom) moments captured on film or disk. If you're one of them, God bless you. Me? I'd sooner spend a week at the opera.

I sent these characters an e-mail with my resume attached, but no cover letter. I was, as you perhaps can tell, only semi-interested. Figured I'd see what, if anything, they would have to offer me.

Ironically, that morning I also had to take care of a

previously scheduled assignment for the Banner. For while the cutbacks were immediate, I still had to get a few photos at, of all things, "The Future, or not, of Newspapers," a symposium being held at Harvard's Kennedy School of Government.

That's right. A photographer from a struggling newspaper going to cover a panel discussion about the future of newspapers. Like venereal disease, irony is the gift that keeps on giving.

The panel itself had its interesting moments. Newspapers will never die, one panelist insisted to applause. Another said that newspapers would go the way of the eight track cartridge, to a somber silence, followed by a few hisses. At Harvard, they don't boo, old boy. They hiss.

Before the hisses could turn to anything potentially violent like throat clearing or knuckle cracking, I began to pack up my belongings. Then my phone vibrated. The number on the caller ID was vaguely familiar, a "Haven't I seen you somewhere before?" number but no name came up with it. I could almost place it but my memory wasn't quite connecting. I was about to let the voice mail take it when it hit me. Once I got outside the lecture hall, I answered.

"Ben Hudson, Detective Bruce Cowley, Boston Police, speaking. We found your business card in the wallet of a brand spanking new murder victim name of Isaac Lynch," Cowley said. "Any bells?"

"Hell, yeah. That was the guy at the toy show," I blurted.

"I believe you can find my office without much

trouble, am I right?" he asked, before hanging up.

"He had a few business cards on him," Cowley told me later as we sat in his office, an upgrade of sorts. The last time I was with him he had a cubicle.

"And his desk and bureau had several more," he added, then smiled. "I never heard of any of those people. But I've heard of you." The smile stopped. "So what can you tell me?"

"I talked to him at the show for a few minutes," I said. "And I saw him at a bar the other night. I bought a Zyratron—"

"It's just getting good," Cowley said. "Keep going. What is a Zyratron and what significance does he or she hold here?"

I explained Zyratron to him and the gift for Linda. I told him how it was later stolen from the trunk of her car, or part of it was anyway.

"Zyratron. Never heard of it. I used to like the Bowery Boys in college, but Zyratron? Nope," he said and started going through some papers on his desk. "Wonder if there was anything at his place," he muttered half to himself. He then turned to his computer and started scrolling through something or other. Nothing. He picked up his phone.

"Sally, did they finish picking up at that victim's apartment? Yeah, the skull. Thanks," he said, then covered the phone before telling me, "Looks like he died from a massive skull fracture."

After a pause he began to take notes. "Well, was there anything called a Zyratron found there." He looked at me. "What is it, Ben? A doll, figurine thing? Yeah, Sally. A figurine thing. It's a kind of science fiction, I guess."

He listened for a moment, frowning a bit. "Well, that could account for some, or a lot, of the paint chips we found, too." Pause. "Different paints? How old, do you know? Yeah. Well, we probably have to test the chips then." Pause. "All of them. Yeah, helluva task but if we have that many different types. Test them all. Maybe they are from the furniture. Plus we found those small tubes of paint, right? Brushes and shit." Pause. "I know. A lovely crime scene. OK. Later."

Gradually, Cowley seemed to grow more annoyed and discouraged as the conversation wound down. As a desperate attempt at empathy, I spoke after he hung up.

"That didn't sound encouraging," I said.

"Hard to know, Ben. Hard to know," he replied. "Of course, as a member of the media, you never heard a word of it."

"Heard a word of what?" I said. We both knew the routine. The way my career was going lately, I was just glad to still be referred to as part of the media.

"Well, there's not much to keep quiet about. Lynch's place was pretty wrecked," he continued. "As was he. Along with blood, there were a lot of paint chips evidently from these Zyratron dolls. Five or six of them were smashed during the rampage. Plus, this guy had a few tubes of paint like artists might use. Some of that was squirted around. Major mess. So we have to be sure that what looks like dried blood really is blood, and not paint. And vice versa."

He took a gulp of coffee. "Good news: the lab has a ton of shit to go through that, potentially, could yield some clues. Bad news: the lab has a ton of shit to go through that, more likely, won't tell us a great deal. Either way, it will take a while. Don't think of it as a big fucking mess. Rather think of it as a lot of little fucking opportunities. That Zyratron could be nothing but we'll see. The lab and techie folks can be amazing sometimes."

I then thought of something else.

"The original Zyratrons—of which there is only a handful in existence—are worth thousands apiece to the serious collectors of that stuff. The one I bought that got ripped off was an imitation; got it for $12. Lynch even gave me a two-fer deal, so I got one too. Not worth stealing, let alone killing for."

Cowley nodded before saying, "Were these figurines kind of fragile or brittle so they'd break easily if you dropped one?"

"No I don't think so," I replied. "Unless someone thought it was an original, saw it was a fake, and smashed it because he was pissed off and frustrated?

"Hmmph," Cowley said, or words to that effect.

Hmmph, indeed. I left Cowley's office and made a mental note that the next birthday present I buy for a woman would be chocolate. This whole thing will teach me not to be thoughtful again anytime soon.

CHAPTER 7

I followed up on that part-time "no weddings" job posting. Or rather, they followed up with me. And it was part-time work, to be sure. And, yes, it did not involve weddings. It was worse.

I was a member of the paparazzi.

But bills waited anxiously to be paid. And so it was that I found myself waiting, camera in hand, in front of Abe & Louie's Steak House in the hopes that TV and movie star Lori Sinclair soon would be there.

No matter how I tried to dress it up, this is what I had deteriorated to: feeding the gossip-churning machinery. Working alongside grown men who called themselves "paps."

It paid $100 per photo, if one was used by any publication or web site. However at the moment I was with three other would be paparazzi. So if we all got essentially the same photo of the same alleged celebrity...who knows?

Now there was a time in the history of Boston that the city would be as much a site for celebrity viewings as it would be for an anti-Irish demonstration on St. Patrick's Day. But in recent years, moviemakers have come to realize that Boston offers backdrops and scenery that moviegoers have not seen a million times already. And the collective political powers have extended certain tax inducements to make it more affordable and appealing to film here.

Sinclair, of course, had been one of the attractions at the toy collectors' show but I had left the building before she appeared. Or she'd left the building after I appeared. Or both. Whatever, we never connected and I trust she has managed to get over it.

My colleagues for the evening were a disparate bunch.

One guy was about six feet tall and wore all black—shirt, jeans, and sneakers—along with a beret, slanted at a slight left to right angle. Somehow he made it work. Me? In a beret, I look like Inspector Clouseau's valet.

The second pap (oh, brother) wore an Oakland A's hat, backwards, and jeans. In his left ear lobe was a very red earring, shaped like a heart.

Photog number three had long hair, past his ears. The only unusual complement was a sky blue streak in his hair, from the crown down the left side as his hair fell in a single bang to his jaw line. Well, it's a free country.

The work-related jargon was unique, in its own way.

"The sidewalks in Manhattan are wider than the ones

up here," the beret grunted.

"The Indians designed the city with that in mind," the earring replied. "The Paparazzi tribe."

Two attractive women came out of Abe & Louie's. The others mentally went through their celebrity Rolodex and instantly decided neither was worth a photo. Me? I'd have eloped on the spot with either one but that would have been unprofessional.

"My brother does this in Los Angeles," the blue streak said. "He was there the night Paris Hilton got out of her limo sans panties."

The others reacted like the guy had said he was there for the Beatles at Shea Stadium. I half-thought that the beret was going to kiss his ring.

"We all stand on guard for a shot like that," the earring said solemnly, as the others nodded in unison.

The beret's cell bleeped and he answered, talking in short, staccato bursts.

"Yeah? Hammersley's? Just now? Huh. Keep that in mind. See ya." He put the phone back on its clip.

"Pal I know at Hammersley's," he told us. "He says that Pedro Octavez just sat down for dinner." Octavez bats fifth for the Red Sox, which in Boston is like being Speaker of the House in Washington. Still, he was unlikely to be traded and would still be here a month from now. Also, he has never been arrested and has been married to the same woman for several years. Definite non-paparazzi material.

"Hmmph," grunted the beret. "Fuck him. I'm a Yankees fan and he kills us every game."

As he said the word "Yankee" but before he got to

"every game," the restaurant doors opened and a flying V wedge of leather wearing behemoths emerged, bee-lining to a town car that had crawled to the curb.

"Coming out. Coming through," one of them shouted briskly, while still advancing. I moved away before the left tackle behind him made an omelet out of me. As the four blocks of granite got to the car and stopped, I saw what I assumed was the still-impressive rear view of Lori Sinclair as she stooped to enter the car. Don't know about sans panties in this case as she was wearing jeans. Kind of a tight fit, though, if that's any help.

"Lori! Hey, Lori," the earring shouted as what seemed like a laser show ensued as we all took what photos we could get.

Well, actually "they" took what they could. Old three fingers Hudson here never got the camera up off his navel. Avoiding Mount McKinley in the leather jacket was the only thing on my mind. I mean, I literally took maybe 10-15 pictures thanks to my motor drive. But they couldn't have resulted in anything, given all the commotion and physical jarring. I'd see later.

The car door closed on her, the four leathernecks jumped in, and the car took off amidst a confetti of strobes and flashes.

Once the, well, shooting stopped, there was a collective exhale from the earring, the beret and the blue streak, who shrugged and said, "Well, at least your brother will always have Paris."

When I got home later, I took a look at the sour fruits

of my paparazzi labor. While Lori Sinclair was being escorted to her car by steamrollers-R-us, I had hit the motor drive on my camera and rattled off 14 shots. I put them up on my laptop and saw that eight of them were close-ups of the bodyguard's midsection; above the belt, at least.

Evidently my camera got twisted around, resulting in four shots of people watching this fiasco; three young women whose expressions ranged from "what the hell" to bemusement at the impromptu sidewalk show we were putting on. All three were viewed at a slanted angle when, I guess, my grip on the camera slipped during the commotion. Maybe I could use it as part of a photo essay on the celebrity saturation of our culture—or some self-consciously titled exhibit like that.

The two remaining shots were close-ups of the forearm of one of the bodyguards. His forearm, roughly the size of a honey baked ham, featured a tattoo of some sort. I blew up the two shots I had of him, or his arm, actually, on the screen and it looked like a tattoo of a gondola. I've never been to Venice, but even I could identify that.

This was the largest bodyguard of the bunch. He would have blocked out the sun, if the sun had been out at that hour. Considering the physical mismatch I faced, I felt a little less embarrassed that all I got was a close-up of his forearm; a forearm that for some weird can't-put-my-finger-on why reason looked vaguely familiar. Must be staying up too late, I mused.

If nothing else, a lesson was learned: as a first-timer, I was definitely not ready to play in the paparazzi major leagues. I couldn't figure out why, but I felt somewhat relieved at that.

CHAPTER 8

The radio alarm woke me with something or other about a hearing at the State House involving a proposed increase either in the subway fare or the sales tax. I was half awake so I couldn't be sure. You know how it is.

Once I got moving around a bit I could actually hear and understand what was being said. Turns out I hadn't missed much. It was, in fact, a subway fare increase that was being discussed, something the Massachusetts legislature has been arguing about since Jack Kennedy entered politics, or so it seems. Also in the news, some corpse surfaced near the Hatch Shell and the Red Sox were opening a homestand later that evening.

Most radio stations get most of their info from that morning's newspapers or the newspapers' respective websites. ("LLB," remember?) Later while I was sitting at my local eatery, Sal's Diner, and enjoying his coffee and a fresh-that-week donut, I flipped through both Boston papers, the Courier and the Tribune.

It was a slow news day, to tell you the truth. Both covered the story about the body that washed up on the shores of the Charles River, near the Hatch Shell. And both devoted about the same amount of space, the same amount of words. No photos just a textbook three paragraph who-what-when-where-how write up, no byline. Except of course they didn't have a "how" or even a "who" as Boston police had no ID to announce. In fact, each paper had the same story virtually verbatim.

After reading, skimming actually, the Tribune's account, I was about to jump to their sports section. But something made me do a double take and go back to the account of the floater. Their last line was different from the Courier. In fact, it was the only really unique difference in the way the papers covered the story.

The very last line of the Tribune read, "The police have no identification to release at this time and are asking the public for help. The victim was stocky, about 5' 9" and appeared to be possibly of Eastern European or Middle Eastern descent. The only distinguishing characteristic was a gondola tattoo on his left forearm."

CHAPTER 9

With the demand for my services lessened due to the Banner's cut backs, I hadn't visited the office in a week or so. Call it a sign of my latent depression or my being a bit chicken-shit, but I decided to visit on Saturday morning, figuring no one would be around.

The Banner shares a building with a couple of dentists, a lawyer and, on the street floor, a coffee place where laptop computer owners frequently gather. The Banner's offices are down a corridor, near the rear of the first floor.

As I approached the Banner's entrance, I saw the offices were open, Saturday or not. In fact, the door was ajar by maybe a couple of feet.

Newsrooms, by their nature, are not neat-as-a-pin atmospheres. Even in today's cubicles and computers era, it's a little more Oscar Madison than Felix Unger. But this was off the charts. You'd have to tidy up for the place even to qualify as messy.

The barriers between some of the cubicles had been flattened. Some desks were tipped over. Others had the drawers pulled out and the contents emptied on the floor. A sloppy burglar will sometimes do that.

I kind of stared around the offices with sort of a "what the hell?" look on my face. It was deathly quiet, I guess you might say. So I never heard him coming. Until he spoke. A knock-the-wind-out-of-me chill went down my back.

"You gonna light the printer on fire first or start with the men's room?"

For a fairly large man, Sam O'Neil could walk quietly. If I wasn't so glad the voice was his, I'd have slugged him.

"Jesus, Sam!" I blurted out.

"You know, Jesus Sam was actually one of the names my parents were considering, or so they tell me," he matter-of-facted. "Cops are on the way. I came in about 10 minutes ago. Used my cell to call and was in the laptop coffee place when I saw you walk in."

"Good. They see me here alone and they might have arrested me," I said.

"Nah. This was too much physical labor for a photojournalist," Sam said.

"Good point."

"Speaking of good points," Sam went on, "or at least good questions, notice that none of the computers was taken. Or at least I don't see any missing. I guess we shouldn't touch anything but have you looked to see if you're missing anything from your old area?"

I walked about 15 feet to where my work area used to be. My computer hard drive had been moved but not toppled over. All desk drawers were ripped open and contents strewn on the floor. After the pay cut announcement—and news that I'd be used only on a per-assignment basis—I took home two Nikon camera bodies I had been keeping there. So there was nothing of much value to me or, evidently, to the burglars.

"If they took anything, it's no great loss to me," I said over my shoulder. I could hear a siren in the distance.

"Screwy," Sam shrugged, as he looked around. "Just wanted to make a mess? And that was all? Maybe it's a protest. Have we recently editorialized in favor of dog fighting or something? Screwy."

The siren had stopped and I figured we'd have the police here any second. That's when I saw it. A head. On the floor. The head—with no body attached—of what had been my free Zyratron doll I got from the late Isaac Lynch.

"And it just might be getting screwier," I said.

CHAPTER 10

Life for me has never been anything like the box of chocolates axiom. More like a box of steam. Consider the last scheduled assignment on my docket for the Banner:

A little more than a week after I almost lost a rotator cuff in the paparazzi mob trying to take Lori Sinclair's photo, I found myself sitting in her suite in the Four Seasons Hotel. The Banner needed me to take some photos of her, to run with an interview Linda Hamilton was there doing with her.

Earlier, I assured her PR guy that we wouldn't run any photo of her with her eyes half shut or her mouth twisted in any strange expression. The Banner is pretty good at selecting the best photo, I explained to him. Not all publications are. If you get some snarky art director who has an incurable case of fame envy, they will sometimes run a bad mid-blink, halfway through a sneeze photo of a celebrity; sort of a "nyah-nyah" back-at-you dig at the glamorous and the famous.

Linda was asking Sinclair about her thoughts on being called a sex symbol at the age of 52. I had no idea she was 52, and neither would you if you had been there. She either wore very little makeup or a ton of it that was very well applied. Having a professional eye for such things, my money was on there being very little.

She had brown eyes that seemed to light up even when she wasn't smiling or laughing. Her dark hair was moderately short and, as near as I could figure, complemented her face nicely. She wore what the fashion week regulars would probably call the simple black cocktail dress and matching shoes, open toe. Her toe nails were red.

The phrase originated before my time, but I believe the Beat Poets would have referred to her as Va Va Va Voom. Or the Rat Pack. One of those hip crowds.

"They tell me I'm setting a new, remarkable standard," she laughed, rolling her eyes at the last two words. "I don't know what it says about our world that a woman older than—whatever Hollywood's age limit is now, 25?— can still qualify as sexy. What the hell, I've been sexy since I was 16. I'm going to stop now?"

More laughs. She had a way of talking. For someone who was all over the celebrity culture, she nonetheless didn't take herself seriously, which in her case was probably harder to do than it looked.

"Of course it helps any 50-something woman if she has a body fat percentage of about five percent, doesn't it?" she asked, smirking just a little. "I am helped by the fact I can get by on about one big meal a week. After all, in today's culture, if I gain 10-12 pounds, it's grandmother roles for me."

I took maybe six or eight shots and was about ready to leave and let Linda finish her interview. But my eyes fell upon a now familiar figure. Lori Sinclair had a Zyratron figurine on the desk in the corner of the suite. At one point, she had to interrupt the interview to take a quick phone call. While she was on the phone I caught Linda's attention and pointed to the Zyratron.

When she finished her phone call, Linda rather cleverly asked her about the doll: "Your first leading man?"

Sinclair broke out in a laugh, when she realized she was being asked about Zyratron. She was cast in one of the early Zyratron movies as a six-year-old primarily because she knew how to scream loudly, she explained.

"Yes, my first co-star," she said, while rolling her eyes. "The actor inside the Zyratron costume had no basic concept of hygiene, if you know what I mean. I was all of about six years-old at the time. So I could only ask my mother why the monster was so stinky. Poor guy had to wear that heavy costume all day so I guess I should give him a break after all this time, shouldn't I?"

She gestured toward the Zyratron.

"Also, I have a certain fondness for that kitschy sort of thing," Sinclair giggled. "Old matchbook covers, for example, and absolutely anything with Betty Boop on it. Stuff like that. So I mentioned it to those toy show organizers that I never did get one of those Zyratron dolls, even after all these years. So after I dropped about three more similar hints, the lard-asses got the message and gave me one of the replicas. And I think they gave me one from the bottom of the pile. Did you see it?"

She walked over to get it and, yes, it was definitely a black cocktail dress she wore.

"Thing has got a few scratches and even a bare spot or two," she said, handing it to Linda. "And the goddamn head is loose. Thanks for the memories, huh?" More laughs. You can't go wrong with a woman who has a great laugh and looks terrific in a cocktail dress.

I took some photos of her with the Zyratron doll in conversation, her hands gesturing. Sinclair looked at me and said, "Hey, get this shot," and puckered up to kiss the Zyratron.

With just the pressure of her lips barely grazing the Zyratron, the head bent at a roughly 45° angle. More laughs.

"Ach! My sex appeal makes wimps of them all," Sinclair said. She tried to put the head back in place, but soon gave up. "We'll get some glue and fix this work of art at some point," she smirked.

I sat back down and let Linda go on with her interview. I wanted to look attentive, so I watched Lori Sinclair, or to be candid, her legs. As a photographer, I'm supposed to have an eye for details. Nonetheless, I realized that in this case staring could be misinterpreted as being rude. Or staring at Lori Sinclair's legs, which might be called perverted, or maybe justifiably perverted, at best. One thing I am not is, well, rude at least.

So I decided I had better stop staring and semi-absentmindedly looked around the suite. I'd never been in a Four Seasons suite so I figured I'd better get a good look while I could.

The sofa I was sitting in was plush enough and soft enough to swim in. The one I had at home was one you could sink down in as well, but that was primarily because the cushions had not been replaced since Larry Bird retired.

The carpet seemed interesting. Maybe if I stared at that for five seconds or so, then a few seconds at her legs, then the carpet... that might work. Carpet. Legs. Carpet. Legs. Who'd know?

As I was just about convincing myself that a few extra seconds on her legs wouldn't hurt anyone, I noticed a tall man standing in a corner of the suite. For a full second, maybe, and not much longer, our eyes met. God forbid this guy thought I was sizing him up. He could have flossed with me before I even knew what was going on.

Nonetheless, I did hold my stare for the second, wondering if I may have seen him somewhere before. At some time. And a recent time as well. And in that full second (kind of a long time for such a stare), it looked to me as if he too was thinking about where he had seen me before.

A bodyguard or security man, of some sort, I figured. He was tall, easily in the 6'5" or so range. His black hair was worn in what they used to call a military crew cut style. He looked big enough to guard Ft. Knox by himself. I decided to go back to Lori Sinclair's legs.

After a leggy interval, I sneaked a quick glance at the guy. He wasn't looking at me now, his gaze off in the distance out the window overlooking the Public Garden. Still couldn't place him. I was going to say the hell with it, but then saw something. And then I couldn't help but stare.

"Ben? Yoo-hoo?" I finally heard Linda call. "Are you still here on the planet Earth?"

I was still here but felt like a latter day twilight zone was beckoning. I was staring at the tattooed forearm. Tattooed. Another gondola.

A couple of days later, that next issue of the Banner came out. With my paparazzi tasks and all, I didn't have a chance to get any copies for myself until the following day. I saw one of the Banner's boxes on the street corner and reached in to grab a few.

I took a quick look at Linda's interview with Lori Sinclair. They used two of my photos—a nice one of her laughing, and one of her with the Zyratron doll. The latter an odd choice, I thought, but Sinclair had a sexy, kind of bemused expression , which made the photo look appealing. As I promised, no photos of her in mid-blink or anything. Fine. I threw the paper in my backpack as my cell phone rang. It was Linda.

"I just got through reading your article. Nice job, lady," I said in lieu of a hello. I'd get around to reading it soon anyway and Linda usually wrote good pieces. The odds were with me.

"Thanks, honey," she said. "But that's not why I called. Sinclair's publicist called me. What the hell is going on with these Zyratrons is beyond me. But someone saw our article, I guess, and broke into her suite. Guess what was the only thing reported missing? And I don't mean the mints on her pillow."

CHAPTER 11

I forget who it was that once described something as a puzzle wrapped up in an enigma. Churchill? Oprah? Someone like that. Whatever it was, it summed up this whole Zyratron craziness.

Couple of weeks ago or so, maybe less, I had never heard of the damn things. Now people are committing felonies to get a Zyratron. And I thought Lady Gaga's career rise was rapid.

Linda was doing one of those Web exclusive stories for the Banner that our fearless leader had asked for. Even though Lynch and GePetto's killings had made the news, nobody else in the Boston media seemed to be on to this whole Zyratron connection—if there actually was a real connection. Could be a scoop. I must remember, they call them "online exclusives" these days, not scoops.

> "A figurine inspired by a 45-year-old horror movie has been the motivation for a series of burglaries in Boston over the last two-and-half-weeks. Victims have included this reporter, a Banner photographer and actress Lori Sinclair whose Four Seasons suite was burglarized in spite of a hotel security staff being on duty.
>
> "It now appears, however, that we three may have been the lucky ones. The Banner has learned that there were two other Zyratron figurine burglaries. In those two cases, however, the Zyratron owners were savagely murdered."

Now there is a lede that should get readers to turn the page and read on. Or click through and download as we techies like to say. At least I think that's what we like to say.

Linda also included a sidebar on the market for these collectibles. The Zyratron market was mentioned and she included some of the observations Giuseppe GePetto made during his earlier Banner interview.

The sidebar also used a photo I took of the real Zyratron next to one of the copies. The photos included a close-up I took of one of GePetto's real $12,000 Zyratrons with the numbers and letter "Z" on the bottom of its foot. Adjacent to this was another photo of the replica, which had no such identifying mark.

It's tempting to smirk a bit and wonder how many Banner readers could actually contemplate paying $12,000 or so for the real thing. The Banner's demographic is not to be confused with that of the Robb Report. We probably had more readers who could run the four-minute mile than could manage more than 12 grand for something. I can't do either one so what do I know?

I was pleased Linda went through the article without using a single "make a killing in the market" reference. These days most media pseudo-wits would have been unable to resist so obvious a pun.

The Banner used a couple of other file photos I took at the toy collectors' event to illustrate just what a Zyratron was. They also used another I took of GePetto the day Linda and I visited his store for her interview. I was just about to put the paper in my backpack when I saw it. Or rather, saw him. The guy. The real tall guy from Sinclair's hotel suite. There he was at the store.

I called up the images from that day on my computer, blowing up the ones I took that day at the store. He was a bit blurry in the background, but it clearly was the same man. No mistaking him with his height. He wasn't looking right into the camera, but just beyond it, as if he was eyeing something on a distant horizon.

Okay, he was at the store. So? And he gave me a sort of a look while in Lori Sinclair's suite. Or at least I thought he did. I am no law analyst, but even I know this represented nothing close to legal significance.

Still, I wondered just what the hell he was doing at GePetto's store that day. I didn't think he was there to price a Get Smart shoe phone.

CHAPTER 12

The thin, know-it-when-you-see-it line between the wisecrack and wiseass is often crossed by one Teddy Kearns, a columnist for the Boston Tribune. The Trib is the more tabloid-ish of the two Boston dailies so, I don't know, maybe Kearns just blends in better there.

Be that as it may, Kearns was writing about, of all things, the Zyratron thefts and killings—specifically the Banner's online scooping of the rest of the Boston media. Count the sour grapes in the following:

> You remember reading the Boston Banner when stoned in college, don't you? Where else in those days could a perv find an SWF into leather and Long-fellow? Now that Craigslist has

The Zyratron Affair

come along, all the respectable deviants get theirs on line so the paper is hemorrhaging red ink.

Only a paper staffed with a bunch of hermit-eating bong-smokers like the Banner would proclaim a story on the theft of some knockoff Zyratron dolls "an exclusive."

Never heard of Zyratron? Neither had anyone other than the kamikaze, jiu-jitsu descendants in Japan who invented it back in the early 1960s. And around here, not until some glue sniffing science-fiction freaks recently began stealing them.

Zyratron was the character in a few old horror movies that were so bad the CIA showed them to communist spies to torture them into revealing information. That bad.

Our Far East brethren somehow managed to convince a toy maker back then to produce a line of Zyratron dolls. In all, they sold about 14 of them. But the originals that are still known to exist are worth thousands here in the cultural

> hangnail of the globe, the United States.
>
> And you wonder why the Japanese still laugh at us under their breath?
>
> Someone has recently been producing a series of fake Zyratrons which a handful of brainless geniuses have been grabbing. And in the process, murdering two of the Zyratron owners.
>
> I don't skip over that last fact loosely, dear reader. But if you wonder why the average person's attention span in America these days is roughly seven seconds—and their IQ equal to that of a sno-cone—consider the priorities being displayed in L'Affaire Zyratron….

The ever sympathetic Kearns threw in a couple more quasi-racist Japanese/Asian double entendres before ending with a challenge to what he called the "Zyratron Pirates."

> Hey, Zyratron-san, I've got two knock off Zyratrons here on my desk. Or maybe it's the real thing? I'll keep one here just

```
in case it's a real one. The
other I'll tape to a statue lo-
cated on Boston's Freedom
Trail. See if you can track it
down. First one to find it gets
a free green card.
```

The mind of Teddy Kearns. Where it's always 1955. Just the same, we at the Banner kind of liked it. Kind of.

Later that afternoon, Sam called and we allowed each other a modicum of gloating.

"Always a satisfying feeling when we little old weeklies get piggy-backed by the dailies, isn't it?" Sam asked. "Not bad for a bunch of bong-smoking hermit eaters."

CHAPTER 13

Sam turned out to be more right than we knew. Not only was Teddy Kearns piggy-backing on the Banner's Zyratron coverage, TV news, the blogosphere and talk radio also started playing catch-up—to Linda's chagrin.

"Shit, they want me to talk to numb-nuts at 7:45 in the morning?"

Linda phoned me that night and was reading aloud her e-mail containing the list of Boston media outlets on which the Banner wanted her to appear ... or "perform," as she smirkingly put it. "Numb-nuts" would be Alan Mann, host of the morning drive time talk show on WGSK-FM called "The Mann Cave," which may give you an idea of the cutting-edge it straddles.

"Oh, now this is great. I'm to talk with Jane Ashton from Channel 9. Another broad with bigger boobs and better hair than mine. Cripes, I'm sure to win that on-screen match-up."

It was the latest example of the modern day transmedia tradition of appearing on TV and talk radio after breaking a story. This sort of self-promoting cross-pollination has been going on for quite some time, of course. Many sports or political columnists frequently write in an opinionated style aimed at, among other things, garnering them more radio or, ideally, TV exposure.

Linda's Banner online exclusive containing additional info on the Zyratron thefts and murders jolted many in the area media. Consequently, she became an in-demand guest for the various outlets. While fairly egoless as media types go, she was nonetheless flattered on a certain level. Likewise, she saw the pragmatic gain, both for her and the Banner, in making the media rounds.

Let's face it, her employer had only recently dropped a financial-difficulties bombshell on her and the rest of us. Getting some attention and publicity for the paper and her articles could only help. More eyeballs, print and online, would be a win-win for all of us.

So it was that the next morning she had to get herself up and going early to call in to the "Mann Cave" radio show. It's morning, drive-time talk radio and let's just say that, intellectually, the Lincoln-Douglas Debates it ain't.

Want examples? Each year on Pearl Harbor Day, December 7, Mann proudly gets in trouble for playing that old pop song "Turning Japanese." Out of loyalty to my co-worker, I set my alarm and got up early enough to hear Linda's segment.

I also turned on my TV. In one of the more strange cross-media phenomena of recent years, some radio talk shows are also televised. Why something aimed at the drive-time radio audience is also on TV escapes me but, then again, a number of things escape me lately. Cheap programming, I guess.

Just before Linda was scheduled to be interviewed, I heard a commercial featuring one of the other WGSK personalities, and I use that word advisedly. The man was singing the praises of his recent eye surgery, saying that going to Doctor Whosis was your best bet. "Do your research before you decide and I'm sure you'll agree with me," he concluded.

I don't know. If I'm ever trying to decide who to let fire a laser into my retina, my research won't involve getting feedback from a radio personality. Receiving a medical referral from them would be like getting nutrition advice from Keith Richards. After the eye surgery commercial, Linda came on—or rather, her voice did. On television, they didn't even run a photo of her, just the Banner's logo instead.

The Banner owners must have really given her an "or else" order to go on the show as I know Mann is not her idea of how to wake up in the morning. But as the interview unfolded, it wasn't as juvenile as one would have thought. Mann seemed to have actually prepared for the interview, asking about GePetto's store and her interview with him. And Linda spoke well and fondly of meeting "Mr. GePetto" as she called him.

A break for a traffic report followed. Then after a few minutes of recapping the Zyratron story and related happenings, the topic semi-shifted to action heroes. "Action," in the world of talk radio hosts such as Mann, meant, well, getting some, er, action.

Or not.

"Our 'GSK Mann Cave online poll asks, 'Which superhero would you want to nail: Spiderman, Superman, Wonder Woman or Supergirl?'" Mann said. "We've got something for everyone there, don't we? So far, 56% answered Wonder Woman, 24% said Supergirl and 10% each said they prefer to nail Spiderman or Superman. Now, Linda, which super hero would you rather nail?"

"Huh?" was Linda's response. The interview was being conducted around 7:45 a.m. and while I guess she'd been up at that hour before, it probably wasn't very recently.

"Or maybe you're a Spiderman chick, Linda?" Mann followed up.

"Women never tell, you know that, Mann," she replied. "But tell us, who'd you rather nail?" She had the radio host's ego pegged perfectly.

"Me?" Mann said. "Me, I'd nail Wonder Woman every way from Sunday."

"Yeah?" she came back. "Five minutes with a real Wonder Woman and all that would be left of you would be the holes in your socks."

Some of Mann's on-air cronies fell apart laughing but Mann himself seemed, well, quieted by her answer.

"Wait, fellas, wait," he said, quieting his troops.

"Linda, have you ever seen me naked?" This was evidently one of his standard lines when he was in a truly witty mood.

"No, and without my telescope I'm told I'd be lost," Linda cracked. All the studio boys with Mann went nuts.

"Hey, who knew Banner chicks talked dirty?" Mann asked listeners. "Someday we should hook up, you know? I could wear my Schwarzenegger mask. With your name, that should get things going, huh?"

"Mann, you little boy, I'd sooner kiss the third rail at Ashmont Station," Linda said, applying the knock out. And hung up.

"Good Lord, bubble gum has a higher IQ than that Mann show and its listeners," Linda told me later. Between her interviews, she met Sam and me for lunch. "The Banner better appreciate my slumming it like that."

"Who knew our little Linda could talk dirty that early in the morning?" Sam asked, holding his glass up in a toast.

"Numb-nuts' producer called me and asked if I wanted to come back sometime," she said, rolling her eyes.

"Hey, if the Banner keeps skidding..." I said, shrugging.

"OK, you," she glared at me, "you'll be under that third rail at Ashmont in a minute. At least I didn't have to get up and physically get into their studio for this."

"Well, I'll concede that having our reporters interviewed about their articles may be beneficial in terms of attracting readership and eyeballs to the website," Sam said. "But I'm worried if the Banner bigwigs would want us to start using those online polls on our site."

"An online poll is a little like porn," I theorized. "No one looks at it but everyone looks at it, you know?"

Linda stared at me for a second before saying, "Well, I never analyzed it through that prism before, Benjamin."

"What I mean is that online polls just fool readers into thinking they are somehow involved in the news," I stammered. "They click on one of the four or five choices we give them and think they're part of the story somehow."

"We are living in the Golden Age of Bullshit, people. It's a new dawn," Sam concluded. "As has often been the case over the years, perhaps Mr. Dylan was right when he suggested, 'get out of the new one if you can't lend a hand.'"

"Uh, I don't think Bob was analyzing online polls when he sang that, was he?" Linda chuckled.

"No? Who the hell knows?" Sam grumbled. "I know, we'll ask our readers. Let's put up an online poll about it...."

Later that day, Linda was interviewed on a couple of local TV newscasts. She sounded intelligent and all that, or as intelligent as one can sound in three separate sound bites of roughly 8 to 10 seconds each. She spoke respectfully of the late GePetto but was candid about Zyratron, despite the character's newly found fame.

"Zyratron wasn't even a one-hit wonder. It is just a tongue-in-cheek piece of pop culture," she told the interviewer, apparently the aforementioned Jane Ashton from Channel 9. With regard to Linda's hair-boob worries, I thought her hair looked better but Linda was accurate in her estimate of the reporter's boobs, a conclusion I decided to keep to myself should Linda ever ask me.

At the conclusion of the clip, the reporter was shown standing in front of GePetto's old store and then walking down the sidewalk towards the camera, talking all the while about the murder and saying, "Boston Police are trying to finalize just how it went down."

The store was still as I remembered it, save for a "Store Space Available" banner on the front window. While the reporter walked past several parked cars, I heard nothing I didn't already know, of course, but was watching in the hopes that they'd use another of Linda's comments.

But as they cut away from the reporter, my eyes caught something. A car, a yellow car. I didn't connect right away with the make or model. The human mind is a strange beast. I didn't know why but I was transfixed for a full second or two. A yellow car. So what?

Nothing. I registered nothing other than the distinct feeling that I should have been registering ... something. Hell with it. If it's anything of relevance, it will come back to me later. At some point.

The jazz legend Miles Davis used to drive a canary

yellow Ferrari. I remember reading that somewhere. That yellow car on television was a—what? No Ferrari, that's for damn sure. Might have been a Volvo maybe, or a VW, I think. So? So nothing.

That night about 10 minutes after I got into bed, I had read all of about half a page of a Richard Stark novel. It wasn't the book, as all of Stark's books are terrific. But for just long enough it took my mind off that damn yellow car. But just enough. To remember. And register.

It was a little before midnight. I probably should say 'Round Midnight in thanks to Miles Davis and his canary yellow Ferrari for jump starting my memory.

Was it too late to call anyone? Probably. Too late to call a homicide detective?

I hoped not.

CHAPTER 14

"So from what you told me last night when you called, and from what I'm hearing this morning, this yellow VW is or was GePetto's car," Cowley asked me yet again.

Linda Hamilton and I were in his office that next morning, a little after eight. Between getting up earlier than usual to listen to a Linda's radio interview, and getting in to Cowley's by eight this morning, my sleep patterns were evolving into those of the work-a-day lifestyle. I made a mental note to consider adding this to the skills section of my resume.

"That's right. When Linda and I left his store the day she interviewed him, she pointed the car out to me. Just as a casual aside and nothing more. Near as I can remember, I think GePetto had made some reference to it towards the end of our visit. It went in one ear and out the other at that time. As I told you, a TV report last night showed in the background a quick glimpse of this yellow VW as the reporter walked by. It registered very vaguely right then. Only a little later did I actually remember."

Cowley looked at Linda.

"GePetto referred to his 'yellow bug,' as he called it, as containing a couple of Zyratrons, I think he said," Linda explained. "I just presumed he meant the replicas and doubted he'd keep any of the expensive ones in his car, you know? I feel like an amateur dipshit for not remembering that until Ben called me last night after he phoned you. I'm the reporter with a notebook and such but ... nothing. It never dawned on me."

"No reason it should have," Cowley said to her. "A passing reference like that? Not at all. Hey gang, there's a reason cops like me give you our cards and say, 'If you think of anything at all, give us a call.' Sometimes that's what happens. Like here."

His phone buzzed at that point, and he picked up. "Cowley," and paused. "Shit, I wondered about that." Pause. "I don't know. Not right now. Let me think on it." Pause. "That could be, too. Okay, thanks."

He hung up and flipped through a notebook on his desk.

"The yellow VW—he definitely referred to it as his car, did he?" he asked us.

"Oh, yeah. He said he kept a couple of these Zyratrons 'in my car, that yellow Volks out there,' he called it, or 'bug' or something like that, I guess," Linda said. "He sort of pointed towards the street when he said that. I remember that now."

Cowley stared at his notes, frowning a little. "Well, interest in the GePetto part of the story kind of cooled off," Cowley mused, "or maybe we just didn't have any reason to release this. But GePetto's real name was not GePetto. It's Crawford, James Leo Crawford. That has yet to do us much good. We ran the plates early this morning. The car is registered to someplace called the Crystal Glow Company of San Francisco, California. No street address. A PO box only. No connection right now to GePetto. Or James Leo Crawford." He tossed his notes back on his desk. "So we're checking into when we can get the car, let alone see what it contains."

Linda, almost reflexively, practically imperceptibly, went for her purse and the notebook it contained.

"Uh, you didn't just tell us that," I said, "or did you? I mean, are we sort of working here or are we sort of being grilled here? Maybe a little of each?"

Cowley thought for a few seconds before looking at Linda and replying.

"No, I didn't just tell you that, Ben. But a ... what's the contemporary phrase? 'A source close to the investigation' told you. Yeah. Might be interesting to see what results from that getting out," he said, looking at Linda who by now had her pen and notebook out and was scribbling intensely.

"No wait," Cowley said, then thought some more. "Ah, screw it. Go ahead. See what, if anything, comes of it. 'A source close to the investigation,' right?"

"Yes, Officer Source, sir," Linda winked.

And so it was that later that day, the Banner, the now go-to website for all your Zyratron coverage, featured the following web exclusive under Linda's byline:

> New evidence may be forthcoming in the murder case of the proprietor of the Yesterday & Forever store in Boston's South End.
>
> Boston police are soon expected to search the car belonging to one James Crawford, also known as Giuseppe GePetto, the manager of the store, who was murdered during a store break-in or robbery. His murder is presumed to be connected to the string of thefts of Zyratron replica figurines. Another murder, that of Isaac Lynch of Allston, is also believed to be connected.

The rest of the story recapped the Zyratron history and the other burglaries seemingly aimed at the Zyratron knockoffs.

"Piggy-back this, Boston," Sam e-mailed the Banner staff after posting Linda's story. Before the day was out, we'd set a record both for click-throughs by readers and the number of times the story got e-mailed.

Shortly after that, the Banner publisher e-mailed with "We're winning with LLB, good people!"

So we were. I think.

CHAPTER 15

The Tribune's headline read, "Zyratrons hiding narcotics?"

As it turned out, Teddy Kearns became the recent "Zyratron victim," as he phrased it. In fact, our boy Kearns had a bit of a scare. His office is actually in his home, he explained to his readers—located in a Boston suburb "far too rich for most of you to afford," he so humbly stated.

Evidently that didn't stop the Zyratron freaks who found out where he lived and broke in.

> They searched the place with the subtlety of a train wreck. These crime geniuses left behind a Waterford crystal paperweight, my brand new iPad, and

my main computer with the hard drive untouched—although the thing was knocked off its stand.

   However, these whip-smart criminal masterminds did take the phony (I can now reveal) Zyratron I had written about last week. In point of fact, dear readers, these psycho midgets evidently smashed the toy monster doll while scavenging around the Kearns compound. So who the hell knows anything anymore? They break in, find the Zyratron, smash it to bits, and take off.

   However, police who came and took samples would not identify for this reporter the white, powdery-looking substance that was on my desk. Whether it was plastic chips or plaster-like residue from smashing the phony doll—or the stuff that nasal membrane dreams are made of—they would not, or could not, say.

   This whole thing could get bigger yet, folks, pending the police lab's identification of that powdery stuff. Stay tuned.

The Zyratron Affair

By the way, it turned out someone went out and found the other fake Zyratron, which was "taped to the ass end of Paul Revere's horse," as Kearns phrased it with his usual verbal polish. "This is roughly the general location where these toy thugs can put their entire Zyratron scheme."

"Powdery stuff?" Linda e-mailed me after reading the column. "The only powdery stuff on Teddy's desk is his dandruff."

CHAPTER 16

A thought for today: never stop learning.

And while we're at it, realize you're almost never as smart as you think you are. But often times, you're dumber than you know.

And so it was that at long last, I became the most recent Zyratron victim; make that a second time victim to boot. Earlier, of course, they found and smashed open that Zyratron in my desk at the Banner's offices.

Here, my car's trunk received the royal treatment apparently in the middle of the night after the day Linda and I were in Cowley's office.

When I went out to the car in the morning, I had that same instantaneous "Did I leave my trunk open?" thought that Linda had on the night of her birthday party, and her car was broken into. But here I had to laugh a bit and wonder just how rapid an intellectual pace these thieves were setting.

For one thing, nothing was missing from my trunk except for a tire iron. For a second thing, if they were somehow hoping for another Zyratron, did these geniuses think I'd still have it in the trunk of my car after all this time? They also jimmied open the front passenger door and rifled through the glove compartment. Made a mess of my registration papers, but that was all. Nothing to see here, guys. Move on.

In fact, the trunk still closed properly and while the front passenger door was a bit shaky, I could still close it and drive the car. And did, to one of my now only occasional assignments for the Banner. This one at the New England Aquarium where some seal had just given birth or something or other. The seals would be the Banner's "What-To-Do-This-Weekend" photo on our calendar page. I was playing in the big leagues today.

I drove down Commercial Street towards Atlantic Avenue on the waterfront and began to keep an eye out for a parking space. I still found myself chuckling, but just a little, at the car break-in. Did these criminal wannabes think that, if I still had anything they would need, I'd keep it in my car? How mentally lame a brain did they ...

No, disregard that. How mentally lame was I not to realize that if they already checked my desk at the Banner, and now my car, there was only one place left.

When you perform a U-turn in Boston, at least be grateful you do so on a two-way street. That was about all I had going for me as a cacophony of honking horns, middle fingers and expletives ending with the word "you" showered my desperate attempt to return to the scene of what I'm sure was the crime of breaking and entering into my apartment.

Mine is neither the most palatial nor tidy of dwellings. Upon entering, I saw a few pair of socks and a still damp towel from that morning's shower exactly where I'd left them—strewn about the floor. I had little reason to expect Architectural Digest to conduct a surprise inspection, so what of it?

Under the circumstances, then, it actually took me five or six seconds or so to be sure they actually broke in. Well, seeing the tire iron from my trunk told me that much. They'd used it to break my door's lock and had left it right there on the floor for me. Considerate.

Anyway, once I gave the place the once over, it was obvious they had been there and let's just say the socks and wet towel display was about the tidiest part of the place. They opened various drawers, dresser as well as kitchen. It looks like they even moved the mattress and box spring around while looking under those. And they hit the refrigerator, looking in the freezer as well as the crisper section. The latter was a joke on them as I had nothing there except for half a head of lettuce and a couple of limes that were there so long they had taken on the color of racquetballs.

Books were strewn about, for whatever reason, as one can hardly hide a figurine inside a book. But they had no reason to be subtle, I guess.

The Zyratron Affair

No need to call a homicide detective about a break-in, but I didn't think Cowley would mind under the circumstances. He made sure my place was dusted on the long shot possibility they left fingerprints.

After the police left, I cleaned up a bit. Then I called Sam O'Neil at the Banner. I told him the Aquarium's seals and our "What-To-Do-This Weekend" photo would be delayed. I told him why.

I then had one question for him. I asked it. He chuckled a little and answered, "Yes. Still here."

Despite my not being able to contribute a photo to the Banner's "What To Do This Weekend" section, the weekend nonetheless arrived and, I trust, people managed to find something to do despite my lack of photographic input.

The highlight of my entire weekend was reading that Sunday's papers. I was finishing up my readings late that night. The anniversary of the Windsor Museum art thefts was upcoming and that Sunday's Courier decided to devote a page to it, specifically a photo layout of the art stolen from the museum.

Thanks to Linda's wardrobe selection the day we visited the Yesterday & Forever store, I was aware of "The Girl in a Fountain." But the rest of them were new to me. I'm sure newspaper photographs didn't do them justice. Nothing like the real thing, and all that. So I kind of glanced at the rest of the paintings.

Mad Magazine fold-ins are about as artsy as I usually get so my interpretation of one of them, something called "Etchings of Sunshine" by someone named Jean-Louis Vigeant, may not be very precise.

It appeared to be a drawing of a few trees amidst rural hillsides. A creek or river was flowing down the middle of the scenery.

A couple of small sailboats floated by, as did a gondola in which a man stood, navigating it while a woman reclined upfront. To the far left of the painting was another gondola, larger than the other vessels—making it appear to be closer to shore. It carried no passengers at all. This gondola was empty.

I'm not sure what, if anything, the artist was trying to symbolize with the empty gondola. But it worked for me. I used Cowley's cell number this time. His voice mail answered almost immediately.

"Ben Hudson calling," I voice messaged. "Me calling you. There's a role reversal. Two points: This 'Etchings' illustration in the Courier this morning has re-booted my memory and I may or may not have something of relevance. When we talk, you tell me.

"Second, I couldn't sleep the other night and wonder if we could discuss that in greater detail. Specifically, ..."

"Etchings of Sunshine" by Jean-Louis Vigeant. I had never heard of him. Well, he never heard of me either. Bonjour, Monsieur Vigeant.

CHAPTER 17

I received a short, cryptic text message reply from Cowley:

"My office. Tomorrow. 8 a.m.—Cowley"

I got there a little before 8 a.m. but Cowley was waiting for me. He wasn't alone. He stood as I entered his office. There were two women with him. One was tall thin and Asian. The other was maybe five feet tall with auburn hair. The tall woman was wearing the uniform of the Boston Police. The other woman was wearing a dark business suit and had a visitor's badge on her lapel.

"Ben, this is Officer Chen and this is Agent Cunningham of the FBI," Cowley said. "Do you have your latest Zyratron?"

"Yep," I said as I nodded to both women. Didn't even blink at seeing the FBI at this point. With all that had been going on, Cowley could have introduced them as Moe and Curly and I wouldn't have been surprised. I put my backpack on a chair and removed the Zyratron doll. Only then did I see he already had one on his desk.

"Don't tell me you're a collector now, too?" I asked Cowley.

"We're all collectors at this point," he replied, not cracking any grin I could see. "Hold on to yours for now. The one we have here was found in that yellow VW of GePetto's." He turned towards the FBI agent asking, "Now have we figured out yet if this is a duplicate or a real one?"

"Cripes, my head is spinning so much I don't even know, with all the fakes and real figurines we think we've seen" she said, gesturing towards the Zyratron on Cowley's desk. "Check the bottom of the left foot to see if there is a number there. If so, it may be a real one like the ones they got $12,000 or so for."

Cowley looked at the foot as Cunningham and Chen leaned over to look as well.

"Z, five, seven, nine," Cowley intoned. He stared at it for a second before saying, "Well, everyone else has been smashing these damn things open. It's our turn now. So what's $12,000 or so when you've got murders to solve?"

With that, he gripped the doll by the feet and brought it down hard on the edge of his desk. It didn't shatter and, in fact, didn't seem to dent at all. He was about to raise it for a second try when the Zyratron head and its left arm gave way and were hanging from the body.

A little dust or paint chips fell on his desk. The head and arm were still semi-attached by something inside the doll. It wasn't held by any glue or adhesive. Rather, the doll seemed to be stuffed with some sort of packing material or paper of some sort. Not newspaper but a heavier type; like construction paper from grammar school art class.

"What the hell is this? Crackerjack prize or something?" Cowley said to nobody in particular.

Virtually the whole left upper half of the figurine was now broken away. Cowley was about to pull the whatever-it-was out of the Zyratron. It was Officer Chen, who got it ahead of the rest of us.

"Oh, Jesus Christ. Careful opening it," she said in rapid fire, almost like one long word. "I see paint. Or an illustration of some kind, isn't it?"

Cowley nodded. Only then did I even notice that Cowley was wearing latex gloves. He began to withdraw the whatever-it-was from the Zyratron, very slowly, very methodically. It gave way after a bit and, being sure not to tear it, Cowley was able to split open the figurine and remove what now appeared definitely to be... something.

"Yeah, Grace, we've got some sort of painted or drawn thing here," Cowley said. "I think."

Paint chips began to fall onto the desk and floor. When he finally had the whole thing out, we saw that it was rolled up after having been folded into quarters. Slowly, Cowley began to unfold it. As he started to open this thing up, more flakes of red and brown paint fell on his desk. Cunningham and Chen took a step closer to the desk. Cunningham said in a voice slightly louder than the rest of the group had been using, "Oh, man, that could be one."

Cowley ever so slowly opened it up and, damned if it didn't look a lot like that Fountain Girl image that Linda had on her t-shirt the day we visited GePetto's store. The room was now very quiet. Pin-drop quiet.

"OK. Let's leave it as it is," Cowley said. "Ben, come with us down the hall and we'll see if we get lucky with yours."

Cowley escorted us out of his office and then carefully shut the door. He took us into an empty office, two doors down the hall. After shutting that door, he turned to me with his hand out.

"I hope you haven't become too attached to that doll, Ben," he said, "because I think we have to take a look inside that one too."

"Suits me," I answered, handing him the Zyratron figurine that Sam had kept in his office desk at my request.

Yeah, I know. They already stole mine from my desk at the Banner. True. But this was another Zyratron. I couldn't sleep the other night, the night after Teddy Kearns' column ran in which he said he hid a Zyratron replica somewhere on the Freedom Trail. I just had a notion.

Like a lot of Boston residents, I don't walk the Freedom Trail very often. It runs through the city and highlights historical locations like the site of the Boston Tea Party and the Boston Massacre.

There is also the Old North Church behind which is a statue of Paul Revere astride his horse. Metaphorically, it made a certain amount of twisted sense that the first place a sophisticate like Kearns would think to hide his Zyratron figurine would be under a horse—as he, in fact, revealed in that column that ran a few days after he hid it. And under said horse was where I found it, after practically breaking my neck, not the figurine's for a change, as I somehow scaled the statue to retrieve it. Score one for insomnia.

I had left this other replica Zyratron with Sam. After the Banner got broken into, I figured his desk would then be the safest place for it. They wouldn't be breaking in there again anytime soon, right?

"I'm getting sick of this whole Zyratron craziness any way," I added, after explaining to Chen and Cunningham where this particular Zyratron came from. "I figure this is another knock off, pardon the expression."

"Well, maybe. But now we're not completely sure," said Agent Cunningham. "We think some of these Zyratrons were doctored or forged to the point that the lines became blurred, literally, between the real and replica figurines. Or so we now theorize."

Cowley stared at the Zyratron I gave him, holding it at arms length. For a second I thought he was going to recite the "Alas, poor Yourick" line from Hamlet. But instead he took a breath before saying, "Oh, it's a violent culture," and brought the Zyratron down hard on the desk. Nothing. The figurine didn't crack or give like the other one.

"Benjamin, I'm afraid this could be a real one," Cowley said, still looking at it. "The replicas tend to crack more easily." He again tried to smash the

Zyratron, this time much harder than before. The head cracked a bit, just enough for him to pull it and about half of the torso away.

"Yup. Another prize inside," he said with what I would call a matter-of-fact tone of triumph. He knew he was right but was also confident enough to act like he'd been there before. No touchdown dance needed.

Again, he methodically withdrew what appeared to be thick, rolled-up and folded paper similar, at first glance, to what the other Zyratron held. He unfolded part of the whatever-it-was and stopped.

As he unfolded it, a kind of creaking, almost crackling sound could be heard. The thing had obviously been in there for quite a while and was making an effort to unfold.

After it was unfolded, it appeared to be some sort of illustration or drawing of some type. As Cowley unfolded it ever so slowly, it began to look like another familiar work; this time, Vigeant's "Etchings" and for a guy I'd never heard of before only a few days ago, this Vigeant guy and his damn gondolas were starting to dominate my existence.

As usual, I was a step slower than the rest of the room. Cowley's eyes sort of widened a bit while both Officer Chen and Agent Cunningham emitted audible gasps of breath.

"Okay, Grace," he said in a different tone of voice than before, as if he'd reached a firm conclusion. "Better get the lab folks up here. Hopefully, I didn't damage this stuff by half unfolding it. But let's play it safe, okay?"

"And should we contact the Windsor, too?" she

replied, and it was then and not until then that things began to make some semblance of sense to me. Almost.

"The lab first," he said. "But have their number ready because, yeah, we probably will be calling them." He exhaled a bit, and then said, "In fact, I'm sure we will."

CHAPTER 18

Agent Cunningham and Cowley remained after Officer Chen left. I figured I was done and was putting my jacket back on. The two looked at each other and it was Cowley who spoke up.

"Ben, can you stay a little while?" he asked. "I briefed Agent Cunningham on what you said when we spoke on the phone. I also forwarded her the pictures of the tattooed arm you e-mailed me. She has a few follow-up questions to ask you."

Fine by me. So Cunningham and I went to yet another office, a small conference room actually. After we entered, she closed the door behind me and as I went to sit down, she spoke.

"I've seen you before, you know," she said in an official sounding tone of voice.

It's not always a bad sign for a woman to say that to me, not that it happens very often. But this was an agent of the Federal Bureau of Investigation, after all, so I suppressed the urge to ask her where it was we met, Rome, London or Paris, and what are you drinking.

"You were at that toy collectors show and auction," she said, before I could attempt an answer. "We actually crossed paths and spoke briefly."

She was smiling a bit and may have even enjoyed what I am sure was the puzzled look I was wearing.

"I'm guessing you weren't Batman that day," I came out with.

She giggled a little, which I didn't know FBI agents were allowed to do while on duty.

"You don't remember me as Lois Lane?" she said in mock anger. "I'm going to complain to the wardrobe department the bureau uses for undercover assignments."

We shared a laugh and if she was trying to relax me or break any tension I might have been tempted to feel at being questioned by the FBI, she succeeded.

For more than an hour or so, Cunningham asked me a number of questions about photographing the man, or men, with the gondola tattooed to their arm. Then she asked a series of variations on the same questions about the same subject. It was a good thing I had done nothing or else I would've felt as if I had done something.

"The significance, if any, of these damn gondolas was out of my intellectual strike zone," I told her. "Seemed a strange coincidence, especially after that guy drowned and surfaced near the Hatch Shell. But with everything going on, I never thought there was any reason to report anything. I mean, there are probably more people wearing tattoos these days than not."

She nodded, somewhat reluctantly, I thought. I already explained that once murders and break-ins started happening, a few gondolas here and there seemed pretty irrelevant and blurred into my analytical background.

"Might be relevant," she replied. "But we are not ruling out anything."

The door opened after a quick knock and Cowley rejoined us.

"How's this going?" he asked.

I wasn't sure if the question was being posed to me or to Cunningham. But she spoke up.

"I won't need the rubber hose for this one, Bruce," she said with what I hoped was a sly grin and not a diabolical one. Looking at me, she added, "Detective Cowley vouched for you, Ben, but this gondola connection—to whatever extent there even is a connection—is something I need to get a handle on."

"No chance the gondola is nothing more than the tattoo of choice among the local fraternities this semester, is it?" I asked.

"Stranger things have happened, I suppose," she said. "But Isaac Lynch and the rest of these people weren't enrolled in college, let alone fraternities, as far as we've been able to determine."

Cunningham stopped there. I sensed she knew more about this than I was going to hear from her. Which made sense, I reluctantly admitted to myself.

So Lynch, too, was into this gondola thing or whatever this was turning into. I thought he had some sort of tattoo the day I met him. And Vigeant's 'Etchings' featured a gondola. So what the hell was going on?

"We don't know," she muttered. "I don't get it. I'm a butterfly woman, myself."

Cowley's eye met mine for a second.

"You with a butterfly, Agent Cunningham?" he asked.

"Er, off the record, confidential info there," she said. Almost blushing.

CHAPTER 19

Stolen art recovered in Boston
By Linda Hamilton,
Banner Staff

Two works of art stolen in 2006 from the Windsor Museum have been recovered.

"Girl in a Fountain" by Renaldo Claravecchio and "Etchings of Sunshine" by the French painter Jean-Louis Vigeant were among six works taken during a daring late night break-in. The other four pieces are still missing.

The Zyratron Affair

The various leads, both here in Boston as well as in international art circles, had come up empty until now. However, Boston police were able to recover these two stolen works due to a series of tips and breaks connected to a string of thefts and related murders over the past three weeks.

The recoveries literally emanated from a highly non-artistic source: figurines of Zyratron, a cult figure from a series of low-budget monster movies made in Japan in the early 1960s.

The recent growth in popularity of Zyratron came from the discovery of ten original Zyratron figurines made to capitalize on what producers had originally hoped would be the success of the Zyratron movies.

While three Zyratron movies were filmed, their original popularity was short-lived; likewise for the sales of the original figurines.

Over the years the movies achieved a small following among film students and horror movie buffs, more for the low-budget, not-so-special effects. The originals were filmed in Japanese and when American actors dubbed in English dialogue, the results were unintentionally funny.

As a result, an entertainingly awful, campish hilarity gave the movies a renewed appeal. College campuses soon saw drinking contests and games spring up inspired by the Zyratron films' unintentional errors and characterizations.

In recent years, the toy collectibles market began paying attention, as well as paying big bucks, for the original Zyratron figurines, two of which went for more than $12,000 at a recent Boston auction.

Also paying attention were international art thieves. Sources close to the police investigation revealed that the recovered artworks were hidden inside some Zyratrons, ostensibly making it easier to transport and/or hide the art from discovery.

Matters became more complicated, however, when the art thieves, or those working for them, hid the art inside replica Zyratrons rather than the real ones. Police investigators remain uncertain whether the thieves themselves confused the original figurines with the knockoffs or if competing art thieves stole the Windsor art from the original thieves, and then hid the stolen art inside the replica Zyratrons.

"A possible double cross may have been attempted," one source told the Banner. "International art thieves, if they themselves are robbed, can't very well complain to the police, can they?"

Investigators now believe that at least two murders are directly related to the developments that led to the art recovery. Boston toy collector James Leo Crawford, also known as Giuseppe GePetto, was bludgeoned to death during an apparent robbery. Police later recovered a Zyratron figurine from his car in which they found one of the stolen artworks.

Another victim was Isaac Lynch, who was selling various collectibles at the Toy Collectors and Appreciators Guild Show & Auction recently held in Boston. He was found murdered in his Allston apartment. Police sources tell the Banner that Lynch's apartment held several replica Zyratrons at one time. Fragments of them were strewn about the apartment when his body was discovered.

"We have reason to believe that Mr. Lynch was murdered due to his connection, however unspecific at this time, to the art thefts from the Windsor Museum," Boston Homicide Detective Bruce Cowley told the Banner. "He also possessed a lot of art materials such as paints and brushes, and we believe he was altering the Zyratron replicas by adding imperfections in order to make them appear to resemble the originals. We doubt he fooled anyone and we also did not find any indication he ever possessed any of the stolen art. But his murderer or murderers left his apartment in such a state of disarray that we may never fully know the extent of Mr. Lynch's involvement, if any, in the thefts. The killer or killers apparently smashed open the Zyratron figurines—real or not—to take what, if anything, might have been hidden inside them. We believe they acted on bad information, as near as we can tell at this point."

This reporter as well as Banner photographer Benjamin Hudson were burglarized and had replica Zyratrons smashed open. In Hudson's case, his residence was also burglarized. It is unlikely any artwork was hidden in either Hudson's or this reporter's Zyratron.

Windsor Museum officials are withholding official comment until the recovered artwork can be verified and they can ascertain what repair work will need to be performed on the masterpieces.

CHAPTER 20

Cowley had phoned, inviting Linda and me to come in for a final cleaning up of any loose ends involving the Zyratron-Windsor Museum goings on. When we arrived the next day, FBI Agent Cunningham was waiting for us as well.

Linda was more than pleased. "Ooh, a source at police headquarters," she cooed. "This beats covering toy shows, doesn't it?"

It's fairly unusual in today's culture to hear someone actually admit they don't know the answer to something. Think about it; if someone is stumped for an answer, more often than not they'll sing-and-dance their way past it by saying something like "Uh, it's hard to say," or "Hey, look it up," or, taking a nostalgic interlude back to childhood, "Ask your mother/father."

So as Linda and I sat in Cowley's office, it was refreshing in a sort of counter-cultural way to hear him and Agent Cunningham team up and essentially say "I don't know" in analyzing some segments of the events related to the Zyratron affair.

What they did know was that the "Girl in a Fountain" that was recovered did in fact come from the Zyratron that was found in GePetto's Volkswagen. And the experts were able to verify that it was the real Girl, too.

However, the other art work did not pass the same verification test. That "Etchings of Sunshine" thing by Jean-Louis Vigeant ended up being just a well-done forgery. That was the one inside the Zyratron I brought in to Cowley's that day—the one I'd found under Paul Revere's horse. It took them a few days to get all this, uh, you know, verified.

In other matters, Cowley went on to say that the late Isaac Lynch had a modest police record, mostly in England. He'd been detained a couple of times as a suspect in different art forgeries, but had never been formally arrested, let alone convicted of anything.

"Contrary to what we thought earlier, evidently Mr. Isaac Lynch was quite the expert when it came to art forgery, if you can call Zyratron art in this case," Cowley said. "And he knew his way around a paintbrush and canvas. He had genuine artistic talent which he chose to use more for copying, to put it politely, rather than for anything original. In this instance, his skills were used to make Zyratron replicas so precise that they'd be mistaken for the originals."

I suspect it was somewhat due to Cowley's vouching

for her that Linda once again was in a position of talking to a "source who spoke anonymously because the investigation is still ongoing." Just so I'd look like I belonged, I nodded my head in agreement every few sentences while Linda continued to scribble notes.

"As for the bodyguards—one deceased and another unaccounted for—we now surmise that they were pretty low-level members of this art theft bunch. We tend to doubt that they were doing anything other than just trying to follow the Zyratrons," Cunningham continued. "That's why one of them was in that Yesterday & Forever store when you photographed GePetto. And why they were at the collectors show and auction. That way they could check out the auction as well as the replica Zyratron models that Lynch was selling—the ones we now theorize he had made to try to confuse things."

"Well, if nothing else, he certainly confused things," I said.

Cunningham laughed, just a little. "Yeah, that's true enough. It did. For a little while, anyway. And Bruce, from what you've told me, the wreckage at Lynch's apartment confused things even more."

"Lynch's place was so destroyed that we came up with a lot of pieces of this and particles of that," Cowley jumped in. "But we were at least able to figure out that the fake Zyratrons were made of a plastic not available in the '60s when the originals were manufactured. That stuff about letters or numbers on the foot of the real Zyratrons? A total smoke screen. Complete bullshit. They weigh almost the same but you'd have to really know what to look for to tell the actual difference."

The Zyratron Affair

Irony and verification merged when it turned out my so-called replica Zyratron that Cowley smashed in his office was actually a real one. A $12,000-plus replica.

"Yes, the one you found under Paul Revere's horse turned out to be real after all, Ben. That's the one Kearns planted there, right? We talked to Kearns; an intern at the paper bought one at that collectors show for $12 and then sold it to Kearns for $50 once this Zyratron case got on the general media's radar, after you Banner people scooped them all. That part checks out OK. So poor Kearns had a $12,000 figurine and didn't know it. The intern's the only one who made money on this deal. Heh-heh."

We all got a bit of a laugh out of that one. And Linda glowed at his reference to the Banner scooping everyone.

"Kearns can make up the loss by selling off that Waterford he bragged about having," I smirked. "He'll live."

"All we can figure is that somehow Lynch sold that one to the intern by mistake," Cowley replied. "Or got his forgeries mixed up with a real one—or what he thought was a real one. Maybe that's why they, whoever they are, got to Lynch and killed him."

Linda was furiously taking notes as he talked. This would be our front page for the next edition of the Banner, due out three days after this interview. There would also be additional stories that would be running as those online exclusives we had all grown to love so much lately.

Both Cowley and Cunningham, and I, for what it's worth, had been calling these gondola guys "bodyguards." But no one really knew for sure if that's what they actually were.

"For starters, we're trying to figure out how they got jobs as bodyguards—or whatever their roles were in this. I mean, other than that they sure looked like bodyguards, didn't they?" Cunningham said. "Frankly, they may not have even been bodyguards per se. We don't know how all that came about.

"Evidently, these guys just infiltrated that toy collectors show and anything they thought was related to these Zyratrons. Like GePetto's store. Remember the one you photographed in the background that day you were in the store?"

I remembered. And remembered seeing him later on in Sinclair's Four Seasons suite.

Cunningham then went on to explain that GePetto apparently was supposed to be some sort of front man for the stolen art. He apparently lost track of which Zyratron was which or tried to pull some sort of a switch to fool the original thieves.

"Frankly, that aspect of all this is a pretty fragile speculation," Cunningham told us. "Or, as a former mentor of mine would say, 'a full blown shit storm of reasoning.' In other words, we don't know why. Completely."

She shrugged a little and added, "The tattoo thing, all in all, was a bit over the top for an actual professional criminal, let alone a ring of thieves. If this even was a ring. Only these bodyguards and Lynch had that tattoo, as far as we now know. Maybe they thought it made them hard guys or something. Rough boys. Or maybe they just liked the way the tattoos looked and that was it. Sometimes a cigar is just a cigar, you know? Perhaps the three thought the tattoos were a sort of one-of-the-gang symbolism. Why does anyone go out and get a tattoo?"

She shook her head a bit and continued. "From the perspective of a professional group of criminals, they were a bit too flashy, if you think about it. In the end that may be why, among other things, they were let go, shall we say. Or saw their positions eliminated, to use corporate speak."

There was a pause and I sensed it was wrap-up time.

"So there's where we stand, if you can call that standing," Cowley said. "Now as far as either of you two being worried, I don't think you have anything to fear or any reason to look over your shoulders."

Somewhere I thought I heard a movie soundtrack go "Dut, dut, duuut." I didn't know we should have been looking over our shoulders. Don't shoot me, I'm just the photographer. But, then again, come to think of it....

The four of us got quiet for a few seconds. I nodded. I was getting good at it. Sounded like this tall bodyguard, or whatever he was, is someone I wouldn't come across in my next hotel suite or anywhere down the line.

"This whole interaction with the Zyratron figurines and of these people—they may have found a potential buyer for the art in Japan or here in the states," Cunningham said, in a that's-all-there-is-there-ain't-no-more tone of voice. "Hence, the idea to hide them in those now infamous figurines. However I have no conclusions to draw as to whether they were being smuggled into the US—or were interrupted, shall we say, overseas—then stolen and brought here. For all we now know, someone in Japan, or elsewhere, got away with something. Or is deeply pissed that his artwork is lost."

Cowley was standing up now, buttoning his suit jacket, putting his pen back in his shirt pocket.

"This gang, wherever they are and however many of them there are, might well have been involved in other art thefts. This probably wasn't their first prom, by any means," he said. "Right now, they're like Gutman, the fat man, at the end of The Maltese Falcon. They didn't get all they wanted, so now they more than likely are moving on to the next destination where they might find whatever it is they're looking for. For them, that's just the cost of doing business. Or look, they might even have most of the remaining stolen Windsor artwork and are sort of resigned to cutting their losses and enjoying what they've come away with."

"After all," he said, shaking his head a little, "for all the craziness and killing that went with it, we only came up with one painting. And no arrests yet for anything: art theft, murder…hell, B & E." He shook his head, still irritated about things. "We can't even find that second bodyguard. Where the hell is he? The tall guy. He's a large man but he's pretty small time in this group's line of work. He could turn up somewhere, or not at all."

Linda closed her notebook and as we all rose to leave, she subtly said to the homicide cop and the FBI agent,

"Well, I can, what-do-they-call-it? Play ball? I think I can help you a little on those bodyguards. You can read it in the next Banner, or we can discuss it now. If you have time."

They had time.

CHAPTER 21

Plenty of time, as it turned out.

I had a ringside seat to witness essentially the tying up of most of—but not all—the loose ends of this whole Zyratron mess.

In a bit of a role reversal, Cowley and Agent Cunningham were energetically taking notes, despite their having micro recorders running, as Linda went over notes of her own. I never saw hands move faster. Presumably, they could both make out their own handwriting when all was completed.

I suppose you could say that Linda, as well as Cowley and Cunningham, were straddling a thin line here. The Banner's cutbacks be damned, Linda was still a member of "the media" here. (If you want to stretch the definition a bit, so was I.) And the very combustible and blurry distinction of where and how a media member should be involved in a story, as opposed to covering the story, was being tested.

I prefer to think of it as a form of horse trading—I know this, you know that, so let's get together and thank you for sharing. This is not exactly common but it is also not unheard of. Linda was not outing any of her sources or revealing any tactics or information-gathering secrets here. I figured that this was a no harm/no foul situation. I also doubt she was "revealing" any actual information here that law enforcement did not already have. Confirming what they already suspected? Perhaps. Maybe filling in a blank or two here and there? More likely. As for mutually beneficial?

Well, the next day's online exclusive in the Banner was such a stop-what-you're-doing read that I figure we were no longer just scooping the Boston and even national media on this. Hell, we'd lapped the field.

New clues, but no arrests in art thefts
By Linda Hamilton, Banner Staff

```
     For all the attention that
the Zyratron-related thefts and
murders have drawn, no arrests
have been made nor are any ex-
pected in the near future.
     Few helpful clues were found
```

at either murder site, according to FBI sources who spoke on condition of anonymity because the investigation was still continuing. And at this point law enforcement officials are not optimistic they will find any of these suspects anytime soon.

"We now surmise that the Zyratron thieves who participated in the various Boston area break-ins and murders have more than likely left the city and quite possibly the country," the FBI official added.

Authorities were surprised any of the stolen artwork was still in the United States and speculate that the stolen pieces may have been smuggled to a foreign country immediately after the original Windsor Museum thefts in 2006.

The one authentic piece recovered last week in Boston — Renaldo Claravecchio's "Girl in a Fountain" — may actually have been taken from the thieves who originally stole it from the Windsor.

Authorities are now speculating that the thieves smuggled the artworks to Japan or somewhere in the Far East, where at least one was hidden in one of the Zyratron collectible figurines.

How or why it got back to the United States is not known and may never be known, authorities theorize.

"It's plausible that the original thieves may have been ripped off by another group of thieves and art forgers," explained Ralph Toluca, an international art consultant who has worked with police in several countries on various art thefts.

Toluca admitted he was "pleasantly surprised" that the one stolen masterpiece that was recovered was barely damaged.

"It's not unheard of but it is still a stroke of good fortune that the museum was able to get the 'Girl in a Fountain' back and in reasonably good condition," Toluca explained. "The forged 'Etchings of Sunshine,' while not so well known, is a work that does have its admirers. That forgery, and an excellent forgery it was, is one that someone probably intended to sell as the original."

Ironically, for all the news the Banner had broken on this story, the police and the feds still did not know a whole hell of a lot more about the original Windsor Museum thefts.

The Zyratrons? Yes. The Windsors? Nope.

The article went on to explain that the most commonly fantasized location of one or all of those Windsor masterpieces is completely unreal.

> The whereabouts of the other paintings stolen from the Windsor Museum remain a mystery.
>
> Toluca shot down the notion that stolen artwork ends up hanging in the villa hideout of the head of an international drug cartel or Internet billionaire, categorizing it as "movie fabrications."
>
> "We're skeptical that these or even most other stolen artworks end up hanging in the subterranean basement or mansion of some anonymous playboy or whatever," he said. "At the same time, it's never so simple that these things get stolen and are instantly sold to the highest bidder. Much of the stolen artwork, let alone the masterpieces, are very hard to fence to a collector or even to another party of thieves."
>
> "It's a conundrum that art thieves begin to slowly realize," Toluca explained. "And

frequently, not until it's too late for them to make a profit."

"Speaking right now, they are probably starting to understand that they, in effect, stole something that may prove to be worthless to them, that is to say, near impossible to sell for anywhere near what the art is worth," he said. "Whether these were the actual Windsor art thieves, or others who stole from the Windsor thieves themselves, they're probably having trouble finding anyone who can actually buy it in large part because no one can really afford it."

"Hey, the global economy is hitting everything: the price of oil, gasoline, diamonds ... and priceless artwork. It's tough all over."

And as if the Banner wasn't killing it enough on this story, Linda also tracked down Lori Sinclair. Given the obsession of some people with the celebrity culture, getting an exclusive with Sinclair might have struck them as Pulitzer material. That is, if the celebrity-obsessed knew what a Pulitzer was to begin with.

Actually, Sinclair's insights, such as they were, into this "tall guy," as Cowley called him, showed anecdotally what a dance of the drunken blind sailors this Zyratron thing had become.

Boston Police and local FBI have also been trying to find a man, name unknown, who had ostensibly been working as a bodyguard for actress Lori Sinclair while she was in Boston filming a movie.

Law enforcement believes he was affiliated with the individuals responsible for the Zyratron thefts and related murders. In addition, it is hoped that this group may have been connected to, or have some knowledge of, the thefts from the Windsor Museum.

Sinclair, who also stars on TV's "Wicked Wives," has cooperated with law enforcement as has her Los Angeles-based studio, which was filming a movie in Boston while the Zyratron thefts and murders occurred.

"This tall guy just sort of showed up with other bodyguards that the studio hired for me while we were filming in Boston," Sinclair told the Banner in an exclusive interview. "We had, I don't know, three security men or bodyguards, what-

The Zyratron Affair

ever. This tall one joined in with the other guards, making it a foursome. And I guess the other three just said, 'Well, OK.'"

Sinclair was not formally introduced to him, she said, but added that "he kept hanging around and the rest of us figured he just belonged."

Sinclair was characteristically glib in describing these men.

"Tell you a little secret, I think the reason the studio hired these men may have been more for show than for actual protection from anything, even the dreaded paparazzi," she confided. "Look, honey, I have fans and love them but I'm not Angelina or Lady Gaga, or whomever. Maybe to just keep a few autograph seekers away while I ate dinner? OK. But the studio probably thought it looked good, you know?"

"Some nights I think I had more bodyguards near me than people looking at me," she laughed.

Sinclair's ribald wit, which has made her a favorite of coworkers and fans alike, also was on display in describing this missing bodyguard.

"They really didn't need to provide a phalanx of protection for me. But I do recall that tall one. I could have done worse than to have gone undercover with him and maybe get some information from him, know what I mean?" Sinclair chuckled. "I mean I loved Boston but after a while even a girl my age needs something other than chowder, right? Oh, well. That's show biz."

CHAPTER 22

I headed home and grabbed whatever was in my mailbox before climbing the far from golden stairs to my apartment. I saw a bill and another envelope with "you have qualified" printed next to the address window. Credit card, no doubt. My fiscal status at the present time did not require an extra credit card so as soon as I stepped inside my place, I threw that one out.

The third envelope got my attention. Some pieces of mail just look important. Like this one. Maybe it was the engraved return address on the envelope: Woodward & Drew, 60 State Street, Boston, MA 02110.

I didn't know Woodward & Drew from Abbott & Costello. But it sounded important. Also if they could afford office space at 60 State Street, they had to have a few things going for them. In that area of Boston I'd guess that a single square foot goes for about what I pay per month for rent.

The salutation was "Dear Mr. Hudson." It read as follows:

"With regard to any possible reward from the recovery of 'Girl in a Fountain,' the Windsor Museum regrets to inform you that they do not deem your role in the painting's recovery sufficient to qualify you.

"While the recovery of 'Girl in a Fountain' is cause for rejoicing, that painting was recovered specifically by the Boston police working in conjunction with the Federal Bureau of Investigation.

"The museum has sent a donation to the Patrolmen's Scholarship Foundation in grateful appreciation of the BPD's efforts in retrieving 'Girl in a Fountain.'

"Also, the Ziratetin (*sic*) figurine you turned over to the Boston police and the FBI contained not an original but a forgery of 'Etchings of Sunshine' by Jean-Louis Vigeant, as you are now aware. Had it been the original, the Windsor would gladly have forwarded you the reward for its recovery. In this case, though, the board has decided no reward will be forthcoming.

"Be assured, however, that the Windsor Museum and its board are grateful for the time and effort you put forth. Accordingly, please accept the enclosed lifetime membership to the museum as well as a certificate to its gift shop."

With everything that was going on around me and the entire Zyratron-related crimes, I had not heard anything about any potential reward. I noticed at the bottom of the letter the notation: CC: Det. Bruce Cowley.

But apparently someone else out there had been thinking of a reward. And I do mean "out there."

One Willard Perry was quoted in that day's Courier about how, for all intents and purposes, he'd known long ago where "Girl in a Fountain" was and feels he deserved his due reward.

"I've phoned the FBI as well as the Windsor people several times over the years about possible clues," he was quoted as saying. "They ignored all my ideas and clues. Art lovers everywhere, let alone in Boston, deserve to know the truth here."

The Courier contacted "a spokesman at the Windsor Museum," who said in a statement-sounding reply, "We've been told to refer any calls about the reward to the FBI's Boston office. At this time, we cannot discuss any details about the reward, including whether or not it was paid or to whom."

Perry, who was described in the Courier as "an international business consultant," evidently travelled a lot, especially to Japan where Zyratron had originated. In his mind, this made him 007 material, evidently. He kind of tipped his hand, so to speak, with a couple of more quotes the Courier used.

"They could have at least listened to me," the paper quoted him as saying. "I saw those Zyratron things on my travels to Japan over the years. And you know, my uncle, before he died, knew who the real Boston

Strangler was. Ask why the FBI never replied to him either."

The article closed with a comment from an FBI spokesman who explained, "The Bureau received a number of pieces of information regarding the Windsor Museum thefts. We pursued all credible tips and sources."

The Courier actually scooped us at the Banner for the first time in a second story. They got in contact with the two people who had paid a little less than $12,500 for what they had been told were real, original, rare Zyratrons. Turned out they were not. These people were not amused to be told of this.

"The police came here and were as understandable as they could be, I guess," said one buyer who preferred to remain unidentified. "They explained how they were unable to tell for certain anymore which was a fake and which was real. Judging by the plastic my Zyratron was made of, they thought it might actually be a real one. But turned out it wasn't. I guess they had just smashed the ones they themselves recovered but they allowed mine to be x-rayed and fluoroscoped. But it contained no art work at all, for all the good that does me."

Another collector gave his name, Michael Archibald. He was more financially philosophical, you might say.

"For what I paid, I sure hope it's a genuine Zyratron. After all this, it's bound to have increased in value," he told the Courier. "I'm having an expert in New York look it over later this week. I won't be happy if I got taken here. There's no one to go after legally. Those thieves have fled to who knows where. That GePetto man is dead. We'll see."

He wasn't giving up on the toy collecting thing, he assured the paper.

"I'm still a collector," he said. "But if this isn't a real Zyratron, I don't know. I could have had the original Lone Ranger holster for that $12,500 I spent...."

CHAPTER 23

While I drank no alcohol and ate no spicy food, that night I had a dream that would have made Rod Serling leave the Twilight Zone, throw out his typewriter and enter barber college.

For some reason, I was sitting on the banks of a river, or pond, I forget which. I was holding a paint brush and looking at an easel in front of me. Evidently, I was painting something or other. I looked up and saw my subject. Or subjects, I should say.

Linda Hamilton was standing on the shore, wearing a dress similar to that of the subject of "Girl in a Fountain," and looking plaintively to me, saying, "Ben, I got to pee again. Take five, please?"

On the river itself (I guess it was a river or brook. It had a current flowing from right to left.), a gondola was

The Zyratron Affair

slowly cruising along with that tall bodyguard, pushing it against the current, so as to stay in place. His passenger was Lori Sinclair, wearing her black cocktail dress and reclining with her legs crossed, a high heel dangling from her left foot.

"Hi, pal," she purred. "First you nail me with a camera, and now get me with an easel. Such a talent, you are."

Strolling by me on the left was the Zyratron figurine which somehow was walking like a normal human being. With him was Sam O'Neil who was explaining how, "Jackie Wilson was a great, great performer of many hits including 'Lonely Teardrops.' He greatly influenced Van Morrison who later had a hit song called 'Jackie Wilson Said.' So what I try to do is get a bar's jukebox to play...."

As they walked on out of my hearing range, Zyratron seemed transfixed by this story.

I looked at my easel to check my work only to see the face of Isaac Lynch looking back at me, saying in his crisp British accent, "Who's starting for the Red Sox tonight, do you know, old chap?"

I then heard a woman's voice off to my right and turned to see Special Agent Grace Cunningham, her back to me, naked from the waist up, asking "Let me know when you need me."

Next to her right shoulder blade was a butterfly tattoo, with bright red wings. A vaguely familiar gentleman in a well-tailored dark suit was examining the butterfly with a magnifying glass.

"Very good indeed, Agent Cunningham. Carry on," he

said, lowering the magnifying glass, standing back. That's when I recognized him and you know you're in a strange dream when J. Edgar Hoover is the most normally dressed person in it.

Cowley followed up with me the next day on a few things including the reward that wasn't.

"Aw, that nut case Perry phones in tips to us or the Bureau every time there's a full moon or his cable goes out," Cowley said to me on the phone the next day. "They call him Bats in the Belfry Perry. Did you read his rant about the Strangler? I hear he still brings up inside info on the Lindbergh kidnapping sometimes."

Switching topics, he said in an edgy voice, "Lawyers can't suck enough sometimes, you know it?"

Cowley had planted the seed with the Windsor people, as well as their law firm, that the info I'd given him throughout the case should qualify me for a reward. The museum had offered a reward some years back—in fact, the week after the original thefts occurred, something I'd totally forgotten.

"I'm sorry the cheap bastards at the museum and law firm didn't see things my way, as far as that reward is concerned," he said in a disgusted tone. "I thought you had something coming to you."

I had no idea he was going to bat for me. I much appreciated his gesture and told him so. It might have been interesting to see whether or not I'd have been allowed to accept anything, given that I'm a member of the general media. On the other hand, when most of this whole craziness was going on, I was being used by the Banner on a per assignment basis. Sort of-kind of still part of the media ... but not completely. I explained to Cowley that I wasn't even sure if media people were allowed to receive rewards for stories they have worked on. Such as I worked on this one.

"Well, it's a moot point, if I can use a lawyers' expression without irony," I told him. "Just so my financial advisors and I can have a good laugh, how much reward was on the line here?"

"In the neighborhood of nearly a half million," Cowley said, and I could almost hear him raise his eyebrows a little over the phone.

I felt dizzy for a split second. "Hmmph," I came out with. "Well, there goes the neighborhood."

CHAPTER 24

With the Banner essentially scooping most of the local as well as national media, the paper's fearless owner became fearless again. More importantly, he celebrated the occasion by restoring everyone's salaries back to where they were before the dreaded across the board 20 percent cuts.

"The ROI on our LLB has been huge, people," he e-mailed us, to great enthusiasm. Even better for yours truly, I was back on a fulltime basis and was able to kiss the paparazzi job goodbye.

"I wouldn't want to go the paparazzi route again. But it's ironic, though. That mob scene around Lori Sinclair that time resulted in my lucking out and getting one of those tattoo photos," I remarked to Sam.

"True enough," he replied. "But while this is easy for

me to say, you might want to keep that job open just in case. The Banner can't break stories on international art thefts every week, you know? And given the ever-diminishing IQ of the American public when it comes to anything related to the celebrity culture, there will always be a crying need for dedicated paparazzi. It could be a vocation for you."

We were celebrating in Muldoon's which was a jumping place on this evening. Well, loud as hell, really; too crowded to jump. Evidently some of the colleges in the neighborhood had finished exams or had finished something worth celebrating. And so they were, in no uncertain terms. Sam had crammed his way to the jukebox and dropped in his money for his traditional "Jackie Wilson Said/Lonely Teardrops" songs. Ever the optimist.

I never understood why celebrating something meant chugging shots of fruit-flavored, 90 proof hard liquor. But most of Boston academia was doing just that. Poisons such as blueberry schnapps and apricot liqueur seem to be getting down-the-hatched all over. Sam and I and most of the Banner staffers attending were sticking to good all American imported beer from Germany.

At one point, Linda wiggled her way towards me through the various student bodies, reached out her left hand and yelled, "Follow me." She reached for my right hand and away we went. I think she'd been re-living college and had apparently consumed a few of the 90 proof fruit drinks that were going around. Somehow we managed to stay connected as we squirreled our way to a corridor near the back which led to the restrooms.

She got to the ladies room door, signaled me to wait and then opened the door to peak in. A tall woman wearing a Boston College sweat shirt came out followed by Linda who said to her, "Watch the door for 30 seconds, honey!" and then pulled me into the ladies room.

"One of us is in the wrong room," I said hesitantly, wondering just what was going to happen next.

"Remember my birthday party and the tattoo certificate some of the gang gave me?" she said. Linda made "certificate" sounded like "shurr-rificate," if you know what I mean.

"Sure. I'm just glad they at least didn't steal that from your car like my Zyratron present," I replied. I noticed that the ladies room was a lot cleaner than the men's room there and wondered if that constituted possible gender bias on the part of Muldoon's.

"Well, Zyratron lives!" she said, turning around, unloosening her belt and pulling down her jeans to show me about the top four inches of her right butt cheek.

There, upper right cheek, was the tattoo—Zyratron, in all its roughly three-inch, full color glory.

"Let's see them steal this one," she giggled.

"I'll get my camera and be right back," I offered.

"No chance, dude!" she laughed, zipping up and pointing to the door. "Show's over. Out of here."

I stumbled into the corridor outside of the ladies room to find a line of five or six women—somewhat anxious and a bit confused as they waited to enter.

"Watch out for that hydraulic hand dryer on the left, ladies," I managed to say. "It packs an awful wallop."

I managed to rugby scrum my way back to where Sam and I had been. He appeared to be even more entertained that I was and as I got closer to him, I began to see why—or hear why as Van Morrison's voice could be heard.

"Finally, Ben," he exulted. "'Jackie Wilson Said' has come on. The damn thing works. Hey, what did Linda want?"

"Just a little final bit of info on Zyratron," I said. "Er, off the record and not for attribution."

"Hmmph. Well, we can't complain too much, I guess," Sam semi-shouted over the din. "Did they ever find out what happened to that other bodyguard you mentioned?"

"Nothing. He's pretty low on their totem pole from all indications," I said. "Cowley says the guy could turn up anywhere, or maybe not turn up at all."

Two days later, I got a text from Linda that read, "Pour a stiff drink and read this NOW."

She included a link which, when I opened it, was to CNN's web site. The headline read, "Alligator killed in FL; body parts in stomach."

"Game wardens in Winter Park, Florida, captured and killed a 12 foot alligator that had been the target of gator hunters for several days.

"The alligator was believed to have captured and

devoured several pets belonging to home owners around Dreamweaver Lake in this quiet Florida town. However, when forensic scientists opened up and examined the contents of the reptile's stomach, they were surprised to find human body parts; specifically, what appeared to be a man's arm.

"Police issued a statement confirming the gruesome find but have no identification at this time. No missing persons had been reported recently, police said. They remain puzzled how the alligator could have bitten off an arm without it being reported either via a police call or an ambulance call. No area hospital had any record of an ER visit, either.

"The arm's distinguishing characteristic appeared to have been a gondola tattooed on the forearm."

THE END

In case you missed MEDIA BLITZ...
a sample follows the Author's page —>

ABOUT THE AUTHOR

Joe Nowlan lives in Boston. "The Zyratron Affair" is his second novel, following "Media Blitz."

A graduate of Boston College, he has also written for business magazines on manufacturing-distribution topics as well as health care and medical device-related subjects. Follow him on Twitter: @mediablitz.

CHAPTER 1

To paraphrase a British philosopher, I'm no longer disgusted. I'm just trying to stay amused.

I don't know, the whole thing seemed like a good idea at the time. Felt like one, too. Just call me beautiful but dumb.

It all started with my taking what I figured was just another photo of just another body bag being carried into just another ambulance. See a lot of those these days, don't you? Well, for me it's a living sometimes.

Then I found out who was in the body bag. And how he got there. Then how many more would be joining him. For a while there, I was wondering if the morgue took reservations.

What can I tell you? If I knew then what I know now ... ah, but wouldn't we all. If Pete Best knew then what we all know now maybe he'd have practiced his backbeat more often and The Beatles wouldn't have had to replace him with that Starkey bloke from Rory Storm's band. Maybe life isn't as tough on everyone as that, but who knows? Let's just say that it's been that kind of month or so for me.

Ben Hudson speaking. I am a staff photographer for the Boston Banner, a weekly newspaper. During the late '60's it was referred to as an "underground newspaper." For a paper to qualify as "underground" back then, it had to oppose the Vietnam War, permit the word "fuck" to appear in print occasionally and refer to females under the age of 30 as "chicks." It was a simpler time.

These days, the Banner features articles that deal with real estate booms (or the lack of) or with the inner workings of city hall. The latter being a neat trick given that the Banner's political reporters usually describe everyone in government as "gutless."

Whatever, the Banner is purported to be making money left and right, hand over fist and ass over tea kettle, not to mention from over here and back. I say "purported" because the Banner's owners, Danko Publishing, would print nude photos of their mothers before releasing an actual balance sheet. Last year, Boston Magazine did an article on the Banner in which the past year's after-tax profits were estimated at $2.2 million. Among the Banner's employees that news went over like the Hindenburg landing. It was pretty much known that the highest paid employee was Al Huber, editor. Al was said to be raking in about $45-$50,000/year, albeit with a very small rake. To figure out what each of the rest of us made we just took it down from there.

The Banner sells a lot of ads to bookstores, record companies, restaurants; but the meat and potatoes of its ad revenue come from its Web site's classified section. Apartments to rent/share, dogs & cats for sale, and

MEDIA BLITZ

most especially, men seeking women, women seeking men, cats & dogs seeking men, along with various combinations of vice versa.

It was one of these various combinations that had the Banner's offices in a state of semi-uproar on the morning this all began. Yeah. Come to think of it, it was a raid on an escort service that started the whole thing. An escort service/brothel, actually. Kind of a quaint violation of the law compared to what would follow.

Anyway, one of the Banner's biggest print and online classified advertisers was a company known as the Push-Pull Escort Services. Their offices had been raided and its entire operation (consisting of the two owners, a receptionist and a staff of 15) was arrested on various charges that were described with words like, trafficking, soliciting and interstate pandering and meandering.

The Banner's offices combine the old with the new. Of the 11 desks in the offices, nine have new word processors; well, new used word processors, you know? Contained in a large low-ceilinged room about the size of a suburban front lawn, the desks are set up so that in order to get to the editor and managing editor's offices, you sort of walk a gauntlet of individually decorated work areas.

Hal Mulrey, the copy editor, has a poster of a large apostrophe hanging over his desk. Next desk over, Sidney Crowell, the film and media critic, has a poster of Marlene Dietrich lounging in a doorway of some smoky Berlin nightclub. Paula McDougall, staff reporter, has a poster of a shirtless Brad Pitt on the wall behind her desk. Brad's belt buckle has a day-at-a-glance calendar attached. Removing a day each morning is among her job's few perks, she says, adding that it "makes December 31 all the more special."

Well, anyway, I could give you more but, essentially, that's my Banner, folks. There's what used to be a decent enough darkroom off to the side but asking what a darkroom looks like is like asking who's buried in Grant's Tomb. Besides, in this day and age of digital, it's almost a nostalgic interlude to develop film anymore. Once in a while I'll use few rolls of Tri-X film. But only when I'm in a retro mood.

A TV camera crew was just leaving after having shot some footage of the Banner's newsroom to use during its report on the arrests.

"Holy shit!" Sam O'Neil, the Banner's managing editor exclaimed. "Cops raiding a whore house that calls itself an escort service. That rates as news? Their next scoop'll be that the stores start getting busy each December."

Sam has been with the Banner since it began in 1968. "As but a wee bit of an intern, I cut the inaugural ribbon on our first tab of acid," he occasionally reminds us. He'd once dated Joan Baez and claimed to have prevented an enraged Pete Seeger from pulling the plug on Bob Dylan's guitar when Dylan shocked the folk purists at Newport in 1965 by "going electric."

Few ever doubted Sam's stories. In fact, it took a bit of doing to elicit them from him. Unlike virtually all media types I have met—print, TV or radio, writer, editor or photographer—Sam rarely talks about either himself or drops names of people he claims to know or have known. He's also one of the best writers around. But, in a field of maniacally competitive pricks, he was neither a maniac, competitive nor, in fact, a prick. All he had was talent. So he continues with a weekly. I have always thought that if he could trade some of the talent for a little of that maniacally competitive prick-quality, he'd be better off. Then again, he seemed happier than most of the aforementioned MCPs. So maybe it all works out.

Sam kind of looks like a guy who was at the Newport Festival in '65. He's got brown hair, maybe half of it gray. It's probably shorter now than it was then; now, it's usually longer than the fashionable length, whatever the hell that is. Sam's not going to be interviewed for a cover story in Good Hair Monthly but he's not one of these guys who still looks like the third Deadhead from the left either. He's also worn a beard since anyone can remember.

If you saw him, you'd probably take him for an associate professor from somewhere. Or maybe an ex-football player — a linebacker, small college division. About 6'1" or so, but as for the weight, you're on your own. Sam, uh, likes his beer and has developed a classic beer gut as a sign of this. But it's one of those beer guts that actually look pretty good, like Friar Tuck in Robin Hood or a hip looking operatic tenor.

He dresses fairly well for someone who doesn't need to. His jackets look contemporary enough; no major tweed addiction to speak of. Nor does he feel so self-conscious about a jacket and tie that he'll wear the two with a pair of jeans. You often see that look in newsrooms.

"Awful, that look, isn't it?" he said to me once as just such a thing walked by. "It's as if he thinks he's still got one foot in rebellious adolescence as long as he can wear a pair of Wranglers, no matter the occasion. Why not wear swim trunks if you want to make a real statement ... although God knows what that statement would actually be."

Michael ("Don't ever call him Mike") Hannah, publisher/owner of the Banner, had just finished an interview with some guy from Channel 6 and was about to start another with Sheila Johnson, I think she was, from Channel 9. They were using the editor's office for the interviews. I knew this because the office's usual occupant, Al Huber, was sitting at an extra desk and didn't look too happy about it. He was studying the box scores from the previous evening's NBA action when I approached.

"Is this where I place a classified ad?" I said.

"Turn around and bend over, I'll place it for you," he replied, looking up from Phoenix-Detroit.

"How'd you know it was a Personal?" I asked. I looked into Huber's office and saw Hannah flooded in those bright white lights they use for TV. I could hear low, deep conversational tones but they weren't audible enough to make out.

"Better you than me, Hannah," Huber remarked, gazing into his office/interview room. "Four TV crews've been through here as well as the Courier and Tribune and a bunch of radio folks."

I nodded. "Well, you can't say he's ducked the controversy."

"Duck it? Man, to him this is better than great sex," Huber replied. "Yeah, there'll be a bit of bullshit about the paper being irresponsible in taking ads from anyone with a checkbook. But what the fuck? Next issue, people'll get it just to get a look at the ads and read 'em out loud to their friends. And people are clicking like bastards on the Web site, I'll bet." He chuckled one of those half-smirk, half-amused laughs you hear in newsrooms more than a little. "There's nothing to duck. Look at him. This is like a suite at the Ritz with Cameron Diaz, JLo or whomever it is you kids are hot for this week."

I gazed through the office glass. The cameraman had just cut his laser beams. Hannah and Sheila Johnson shook hands and then Hannah lit a cigarette for himself, then Johnson's. Both exhaled gusts contentedly.

"Uh-huh," I said.

"What I am asking you, sir, is how you can possibly expect me to believe that as publisher of the Banner, you can express any shock or surprise whatsoever over something like the arrest today of one of your advertisers, when the ad in question features a photograph of a barely clad woman, licking a telephone, under the headline reading 'Discretion Assured. Satisfaction Guaranteed?'"

For Alan Mosley, host of WLHL's cleverly named "The Alan Mosley Show," that was a quick, to-the-point question. I had been listening to him for more than two hours before he finally got around to Hannah. A three-hour show, Mosley had spent the first two hours interviewing one Janet Montcrief, author of a book whose title I did not get, but something about college students hooking up for sex between classes. After five minutes I was bored. After 10, I wondered if re-enrolling was in my budget for the fiscal year.

By the time Hannah got on, it made for a

strangely appropriate segue. Hannah was basically paraphrasing what he had told the media that afternoon. "We accept a very wide range of advertisers.... We leave it to the intelligence and discretion of our readers to determine which of our advertisers to patronize...."

For most of the show, Mosley seemed to be the type who wouldn't get too worked up one way or the other over this subject. I mean, earlier, he seemed downright amused at the rate of sex on campus, issuing comments like, "Hell, why do you think I went to BU, huh? Best seven years I ever spent."

Anyway, once Hannah finished giving the Banner's party line on advertisers, Mosley, profile in consistency, turned into a combination Pat Robertson-meets-Wolfman Jack.

"I ask you, sir, again," Mosley intoned. "This woman, with more than half her expansive chest pouring out of her top, is licking the receiver of the telephone and you actually keep a straight face while telling us of your surprise at hearing of your advertiser's actual line of business?"

For the next 15-20 seconds, Hannah could do little better than give his variation of Ralph Kramden's, "Well I felt, er ... hummina, hummina, hummina ... that our, that is the Banner's readership ... hummina, hummina, hummina...." It went downhill from there. Clearly, Defendant Hannah had expected a more sympathetic hearing from Judge Mosley.

"So if an advertiser's money is good," Mosley submitted, "they're allowed in your paper?"

"Yes, in general," Hannah answered. It had been his most complete response so far.

"Interesting," Mosley clucked. "Let's see what Ed

in West Roxbury has to say. Go ahead, Ed. You're on the Alan Mosley Show."

"Yeah, hi, Alan," the caller said. "Is the guy from the Banner there?"

"He's here, Ed," Mosley replied. "What's your comment or question, please?"

"Yeah, well, listen you slime sucking piece of..." For almost 10-15 seconds, the radio audience heard nothing but the WLHL jingle. After some of the singers went through a couple of repetitions of "WLHL: The Spirit of Boston," Mosley finally came back on.

"Well, look, this is obviously something that touches a nerve with some of our listeners," Mosley said, "but we do ask, when you call, that you please be as civil as possible. Still, Mr. Hannah, Ed did indirectly raise a good point about the role of the media and morality, or a lack of. Perhaps we can pursue it after we take this break."

By the time the hour with Mosley was up, I think Hannah's attitude about being in the glare of the spotlight had done a turnaround and the term "media recluse" was a career move he'd soon be considering.

I was driving along Massachusetts Avenue near Symphony Hall. It was a little after 11 p.m. on a Tuesday. Boston was quiet. Once in a while you'd hear a car horn. Maybe. It bordered on downright eerie. Boston without horns honking is like TV with the sound off.

I look like nobody you'd look at twice unless you had nothing else to do. And if you saw me with a few cameras strapped over my shoulders, you'd probably have something better to do. Which is actually a pretty good asset for a photographer. In cities, at least, a guy with a camera or two isn't that unusual a sight.

What else do you want to know? I'm about 6'2" last time I was measured. I played some basketball in high school and kept at it in intramurals in college. Not that I then developed any great perspective on life or anything, but soon I reached a point where even I had better things to do than throw a ball through a hoop. I just found I couldn't improve any, no matter what I did. So now I play once in a great while at a local YMCA.

The problem at the Y is you got these yokels who don't yet know that they can't get any better and that the NBA isn't going to call them. Nonetheless they play each game as if it's Lakers-Celtics, circa. '84. Cough near them and they'll grunt "Got hit!" to call a foul. Conversely, if they straighten out one of your ribs trying to block your shot, and you can manage enough breath to call it, they act as if you just smashed into their new car. ("How can that be a foul!?") You know, we're supposed to "play" basketball, not treat it like war maneuvers. It takes a lot to ruin basketball for me but these types do it. So I play just enough to maintain my girlish figure and that's it.

I got hair, black. I wear glasses, semi-horned rim, sort of half-way between Buddy Holly and Steve Allen. I couldn't grow a beard if there was money in it for me. I almost did once and it didn't look bad for a 14 year-old kid. I, alas, was 25 at the time, so....

The Mosley show was over. So as I drove I listened to the police radio. I have one inserted into the dash the way others have CD players. I traveled a four block course around the Symphony Hall area for the past hour or so, "doing laps," as it were.

MEDIA BLITZ

Two nights a week I freelance for a wire service here in town. I get paid by the photo for anything they choose to publish. If they don't use anything, I am guaranteed a stipend for the two nights. "Stipend." As in "Brother, can you spare a stipend?"

The police band had nothing more exciting to offer than a car alarm somewhere in the North End that wouldn't stop screaming and a call about a loud party in Allston. Having lived there for several years, I can tell you that a loud party in Allston is about as unusual as finding salt in the ocean.

So it was looking more and more like I'd be taking the collar for the night. Then as I turned onto Huntington for about the 23rd time that evening, a call went out for a cruiser and ambulance to head to the Broadway T stop to check on a report of a person falling under a train. (The subway system here is formally called the Massachusetts Bay Transportation Authority — or "The T" for short, which is about the only time-saving concept they've come up with over the years.)

One of the problems in moonlighting like this was that I found myself actually hoping for something bad to happen; some sort of fire, accident, violent crime. The chances are great, of course, that for some sort of scene to take place someone is going to have to be injured or killed... or at least be thoroughly inconvenienced.

It took me barely five minutes to make it to the Broadway stop, which is in South Boston. Judging from the number of blinking red and blue lights there ahead of me, someone had very definitely been inconvenienced. At least.

A cop whose name I didn't get was keeping any

media from descending to the subway platform. He was more or less cornered by a dozen or so people consisting of local residents, passersby and a few media types. I could only get every other word he was saying.

"... Enter as soon as we finish ... fell or pushed, we're not certain ... identification yet ... room for the ambulance, make room for the ambulance, please."

I nodded to Nate Green, a cameraman from Channel 6 and some other guy I didn't know who had a press badge hanging from his suit jacket pocket.

Nate was carrying his video camera. Those things always feel heavier than they look. I know. I took a night course at Edison College last summer about operating one of those. As a night alumnus of the school, I can still rent one of them when available. I figure it's something to add to my list of career options, even though I've listed it just above perfecting my curve ball in terms of its potentially leading to anything.

Even though it was near midnight on a rainy Tuesday, a crowd of, I don't know, 40-50 had come out of nearby homes. Others stood in the doorways of bars with names like "Your Mother's Claddagh" and "The Irish Rose." Ever watch a ball game and see how the crowd reacts if the TV camera swings their way? A comparable psychological mechanism is triggered by the flashing lights on an ambulance or cruiser. I mean no one was or yelling "Hi, Mom," to the cruiser or anything. But a similar sort of moth-to-a-flame attraction results. (Rough draft of e-mail to late philosopher Marshall McLuhan, c/o Great Beyond, please forward. Dear Marshall: Why people wave to camera? Same psychological reaction as when drawn to flashing police light? Appreciate any thoughts. Suggest consult with Sig

Freud on this. Also, interested in your thoughts on Great Beyond, if, in fact, said Beyond exists. And if so, is it all that Great? Regards, Hudson.)

I took half a dozen shots of the crowd mingling in front of the station. If the night was slow enough, maybe the wire would be desperate enough to use it.

Somebody shouted "Here we go!" and from the entrance came three uniformed police followed by two EMTs carrying an unfolded stretcher. "We got a false alarm, maybe?" I heard Nate ask. Before I could chime in with "Guess so," or some such pearl, the crowd murmur came to an abrupt, silenced halt.

From the subway exit came a drab gray fully loaded body bag, with four EMTs doing the heavy lifting.

"It's official," I said to nobody in particular. The bag was being carried to an ambulance parked about 20 feet away to my left. I headed for a point halfway between the subway exit and the ambulance. I shot away and only then became aware that mine was not the only flash going off. I figured the other flash had to be Mike Bridgeman of the Tribune. I'll give you more on him later.

In a surprisingly fluid motion the EMTs hefted the body bag into the ambulance, slammed the rear doors and took off, siren screaming. Why they had to use the siren to take a dead body to a hospital morgue is something the police didn't explain. What they did explain a little later at the press briefing was more interesting.

"The deceased was a Caucasian male who has been identified as one Alan Mosley...."

Made in the USA
Middletown, DE
17 October 2015